"Remember how you once told me 'next time'..."

"And you told me there never would be a next time—that I would never find pleasure in your arms." Sienna's voice was terse and bitter.

Alexis shrugged carelessly. "So I was wrong," he said savagely. "Will your body react differently to mine because you know the truth?"

"You married me because you felt it was your duty! I shall never live with you again as your wife."

His mouth curled, something dark leaping to life in his eyes. "Then I pray that you are already carrying my son. Otherwise...."

"Otherwise?" Sienna taunted him. "Will you take me as you accused my brother of taking your sister?"

"There will come a time when your body will cry out for mine. You'll come to me."

Never!

Books by Penny Jordan

HARLEQUIN PRESENTS
471—FALCON'S PREY
477—TIGER MAN
484—MARRIAGE WITHOUT LOVE
489—LONG COLD WINTER
508—NORTHERN SUNSET
517—BLACKMAIL
519—THE CAGED TIGER
537—DAUGHTER OF HASSAN
553—AN UNBROKEN MARRIAGE
562—BOUGHT WITH HIS NAME
569—ESCAPE FROM DESIRE
584—THE FLAWED MARRIAGE
591—PHANTOM MARRIAGE
602—RESCUE OPERATION
609—DESIRE'S CAPTIVE
618—A SUDDEN ENGAGEMENT
633—PASSIONATE PROTECTION
641—ISLAND OF THE DAWN
650—SAVAGE ATONEMENT
655—MAN-HATER
667—FORGOTTEN PASSION
706—SHADOW MARRIAGE
713—THE INWARD STORM
728—RESPONSE

These books may be available at your local bookseller.

For a list of all titles currently available,
send your name and address to:

Harlequin Reader Service
P.O. Box 52040, Phoenix, AZ 85072-2040
Canadian address: P.O. Box 2800, Postal Station A,
5170 Yonge St., Willowdale, Ont. M2N 5T5

PENNY JORDAN

response

Harlequin Books

TORONTO • NEW YORK • LONDON
AMSTERDAM • PARIS • SYDNEY • HAMBURG
STOCKHOLM • ATHENS • TOKYO • MILAN

Harlequin Presents first edition October 1984
ISBN 0-373-10728-5

Original hardcover edition published in 1984
by Mills & Boon Limited

CHAPTER ONE

SIENNA saw him walk past her office as she paused to fit a new sheet of paper into her typewriter, and even though it was merely his outline she saw through the frosted glass she was interested enough to turn discreetly in her chair and pull open one of the filing cabinet drawers so that she would be facing the door should he decide to walk in. He paused outside, no doubt studying the notice on the door, and Gillian, who owned and ran the agency, crossed her fingers and hissed across at her, 'Here's hoping!'

Her wish was granted. The door opened inwards smoothly and Sienna had a handful of seconds to assimilate the powerful combination of a face that was distinctively hard-boned, its sensual impact deeper by far than any mere handsomeness, before amused grey eyes rested with brief comprehension on her half parted lips and dazed expression.

'Miss Forbes?'

He was addressing Gillian, who smiled and looked equally dazed, leaving Sienna free of his careless scrutiny and at leisure to admire the way the dark wool suit fitted his broad shoulders and to note the leisurely grace with which he folded his tall frame into the chair Gill indicated.

'Your agency has been recommended to me by an acquaintance,' Sienna heard him saying as he extracted a small piece of cardboard from his wallet and handed it across to Gillian. 'I'm in London on business, and unfortunately my secretary's mother has been taken ill and she has had to fly back to New York. I can't cancel the business meetings I've arranged, and I'm hoping you're going to be able to supply me with an adequate replacement. I understand you specialise in multi-lingual secretaries with excellent shorthand and typing speeds. I appreciate that it's short notice, but. . . .'

As she turned back to her typewriter Sienna's fingers trembled, and she witnessed their betrayal with a certain amount of wry self-mockery. She had been working for Gillian for six months. Before that she had worked at home, translating her father's books, doing his research, typing his manuscripts. . . . She sighed. Her father's death had been a sad but not totally unexpected blow. Gerald King had had a weak heart for years, and as her brother Rob had reminded her at the funeral, he had had a very good innings. 'Dad was over seventy, Sienna,' he had told her gently, 'and this is the way he would have wanted to go— quickly and relatively painlessly.'

Sienna knew that Rob was right, but she still missed her father. She had worked with him since she left university, quite content with the calm flow of life in the sleepy Cotswold village where they lived. Gerald King was an expert on Mediaeval history and had taught at the local university prior to his retirement. His books were always well received in academic circles, and Sienna knew with hindsight that Rob was right when he claimed that her life with their father had been at times an unnatural one for a girl in her early twenties. But now that was all over. There had been sufficient money for her to stay on in Waterford-on-the-Hill had she wished, living in the cottage which was

willed to Rob and herself jointly, but Rob had told
her that she was far too young to bury herself
away in the sleepy Cotswold backwater, and it was
at his suggestion that she had taken the job with
Gillian working for her agency as a freelance
temporary secretary. It was her private belief that
Gillian and Rob were in love, but neither of them
seemed prepared to admit it.

Rob was a busy foreign news reporter working
for one of the national papers, and he had met
Gillian at university. Four years older than she
was herself, Rob had always seemed very much the
older brother during her teens, but nowadays they
met as equals and there was a growing bond
between them. Although he scoffed at it, Sienna
considered that her brother was more like their
father than he realised. In Sienna's eyes her father
had always possessed a quality she could only
describe as 'gentlemanly'—nothing to do with
birth, accent, or academic achievements, but
something that went much deeper than that, an
old-fashioned gallantry and consideration for
other people that everyone around him responded
to, and Rob possessed it as well. He might prefer
to assume the role of the hard-bitten tough
journalist, but Sienna had seen him when he
thought himself unobserved, helping others with
that same quiet, almost self-effacing manner which
characterised their father.

Only last night he had challenged her to deny
that he had been right when he insisted that she
come to London, and she had been forced to
admit that he was. He had been on the point of
leaving to cover another story and they had met
briefly in the hall of his flat where she was staying
until she was able to find somewhere for herself.

She had often wondered if having her living with him cramped his style. There was no evidence that the flat had ever been shared with anyone else, but Rob was a virile and very attractive man of twenty-eight and she was not naïve enough to assume that as his sister she was the only female in his life, or that he would restrict himself to chaste goodnight kisses outside his dates' homes.

She came to, with a start, realising that she had been completely lost in her thoughts, flushing to find herself being scrutinised by two pairs of eyes, Gillian's rather puzzled and her companion's openly amused. But it was an amusement that was shot through with something else; and a something else that made her blood tingle, a curious heady excitement spiralling through her body. She had experienced sexual chemistry before, for heaven's sake, Sienna chided herself, but she was forced to admit, rather ruefully, that it had never before been as potent as this. Something she had once read flashed briefly through her mind '. . . she would have followed him to the ends of the earth dressed only in her petticoat. . . .' Someone had once written that about Mary, Queen of Scots and her love for charismatic and dangerous Bothwell, and in that instant, as her sherry-brown eyes met comprehending mocking grey ones, Sienna knew exactly how Mary had felt.

'Mr Stefanides needs a multi-lingual secretary to work for him while he's in London, Sienna,' Gillian repeated. 'I've just told him you're the only girl we have free at the moment. . . .'

'You want me?'

The moment the words left her lips, Sienna flushed pink with mortification. Heavens, did she need to make herself sound even dumber than she most undoubtedly looked?

'If you are agreeable.' The grey eyes darkened an unmistakable message in their depths, leaving her more flustered than she had been before. Her pulse started to thud heavily under her skin, her fingers automatically lifting to the hollow at the base of her throat, toying with the gold chain she always wore, the breath leaving her lungs on a stifled gasp as lean brown fingers reached out, touching the chain, examining the gold medallion suspended from it. Just for a second his fingers brushed against her skin and the whole world seemed to tremble. 'Apollo, the sun god. Did you buy this in Greece?'

It was an idle, almost absent question, and perfectly feasible, because the medallion was exactly the sort of thing a discerning tourist might bring back from a Greek holiday, but as he let the gold drop back against her skin, still warm from his touch, Sienna shook her head, too bemused by the feelings surging up inside her to concentrate properly on what she was saying.

'It was a gift,' she managed, wondering if her tongue really had swollen so much that it made it difficult for her to talk, or if there was some other reason for the husky uncertainty of her voice. 'My brother brought it back for me last year.'

He took a step back and she wondered why she should suddenly feel such a chill, as though the warmth of the sun had suddenly been removed from her body. She glanced out of the window, half expecting to see that the cool April sunshine had given way to cloud and was faintly bemused to see that it hadn't.

'Sienna, Mr Stefanides would like you to go

with him now,' Gill was saying, but his smooth, accentless voice cut into her words, his 'Alexis, please,' bringing a delicate pink to Gillian's cheeks as well as her own. 'My car is on a meter,' he added, glancing at his watch, the wafer-fine broad gold strap catching Sienna's eye, and her stomach muscles clenched down against the sudden surge of desire to see more of his body than the few inches of muscles and dark tanned skin exposed beneath the immaculate cuff of his shirt. What on earth had happened to her?

Through her bewilderment she managed to retain enough of a hold on sanity to be wryly amused at her own reaction. Heavens, she hadn't thought it was possible for her to experience this ... this intensely physical desire for a man that went far beyond merely looking at him and finding him attractive. It was all she could do to prevent herself from reaching out and touching him, from telling him her most intimate thoughts and desires. She found herself mentally stripping him as she listened to the arrangements he was making, her scrutiny of him in no way lustful, but a silent adoration of the male beauty she knew with some deep-seated instinct his clothes cloaked. When he left she managed to croak something; some response which she hoped didn't betray the disorder of her senses, and when he had gone she sank back down into her chair, her brown eyes wide and dazed, her whole body strangely weak.

'Phew!' Gillian rolled her eyes and grinned, 'That's what I call a man! You know who he is, don't you?' she demanded, suddenly practical, too excited to notice Sienna's lack of response. 'He's only Hellas Holidays! Do this job well, Sienna, and the agency could be made! You heard him say we were recommended to him—now if we can get him to recommend us to his millionaire friends. Just think, working on board someone's huge yacht, flying over to Athens to take half an hour's dictation. . . . Hey, dreamer,' she chided gently, 'wake up! Where were you?'

Sienna flushed vividly, wondering what on earth her friend and employer would say if she admitted exactly where she had been, which was in bed with Alexis Stefanides. She was still totally bemused by the whole thing. She had never, ever met a man who generated such a reaction inside her. Oh, she had had boy-friends, but none of them had ever been serious and never in a thousand lifetimes had she ever imagined or wanted to imagine the sort of intimacies with them that her body seemed to crave to share with the tall Greek.

'Pull yourself together, he'll be back in five minutes. He wants you to go straight to the Savoy with him—he's got a suite there, apparently. And he's paying well. Just at the right time too. I haven't got anything else for you for the rest of the week. Just pray that his business keeps him in London for at least a few days,' Gill told her. 'We could do with the money.'

A few days! Sienna shivered, suddenly over-whelmed by the intensity of her reactions. She felt hot and cold, shivery and excited, her brown eyes glittered feverishly in the triangular piquancy of her face, her blonde hair—the only thing she had inherited from her Scandinavian mother—curled softly on to her shoulders, her slender, five-foot-five frame trembling visibly as she tried to control her rioting emotions. It had happened, something she had never dreamed would ever happen. She had fallen in love at first sight.

She shivered again, trying to tell herself she was being stupid; that her reactions were totally ridiculous, reminding herself that she wasn't a teenager but a woman, but it was no good. Something elemental and deep-rooted inside her had sprung to life and she knew with an instinct that overrode caution and common sense that this feeling which had suddenly overwhelmed her was what she had been born for; pre-ordained in her fate, unavoidable; Nemesis, and on that thought she surrendered herself to it, trying and failing to banish from her mind tantalising thoughts of Alexis Stefanides kissing her, touching her, her flesh quivering deliciously as she remembered the brush of his fingers against her skin. And she was the girl several of her dates had dismissed as cold and frigid! It almost made her want to laugh aloud, but then hadn't she too half agreed with them, thinking that physical desire and passion were emotions she was incapable of feeling. And now this torrent of feeling and need; this hunger and total abandonment of pride that would take her to his side at the slightest indication that that was where he wanted her to be.

A sudden thought struck her, her lips forming the words almost before she was ready. 'Is he married?'

Gillian frowned. 'Where have you been? Don't you read your papers? No, he isn't,' she relented, seeing her face. 'But, honey, if you're thinking what I think you're thinking—forget it. I know he looks like the archetypal Greek god, but he's all too human. He also has a reputation for being cruel and arrogant. He's notorious for his women, Sienna, but when he marries I suspect it will be to a girl of his own race; a dutiful Greek virgin.' She held up her hand. 'Okay, I know, or at least I suspect, you qualify on one count, and I can see the effect he's had on you. I don't blame you, honey, he is pretty overwhelming, but you're Rob's sister, and in many ways a little innocent still. . . .'

'I'm twenty-four,' Sienna reminded her dryly, 'two years younger than you.' She broke off as she saw Alexis Stefanides returning, picking up her handbag and taking her coat off the stand by the door, hoping she looked more composed than she felt, ready to match his social smile with one of her own, but when he opened the door, he simply stared at her, and there was such hunger and open desire in the unsmiling look he gave her that her insides turned to jelly. It was as though his body spoke to hers and hers replied in a language that was beyond words. 'I want you,' he said, and hers replied, 'I know, and your wanting is mine.'

'Ready?' Now he smiled, but at Gill, not her. 'I'm not sure how long this will take, but you can invoice me at this address when I return Sienna to you.' He handed her a piece of paper with an address written on it and then held open the door so that Sienna could precede him through it. His hand on the small of her back seemed to burn right through the thin wool suit she was wearing. Rob had insisted on her buying an entire new outfit when she came to London, and this just off-white neat, collarless jacket, cropped short at the waist with its complementary softly pleated skirt had been one of her first buys. It was by Alexon, and although Gillian had directed her towards the Separates Section of the large London stores, Sienna had soon discovered that she had a natural sense of taste and flair for clothes, although she had been careful to bear in mind that hers was the wardrobe of an executive secretary and must reflect that image. At home she had nearly always worn pleated skirts and toning jumpers from Country Casuals, the same sort of clothes her mother had always chosen when she had been a university lecturer's wife.

Kristal King had died when Sienna was fourteen. She had missed her mother dreadfully at first, but she had already been a boarder at the school her parents had chosen for her and gradually she learned to live with her loss. Now suddenly, following Alexis Stefanides out into the brilliant spring sunshine, she wished very badly that she was alive, wanting someone to talk to about the wholly unexpected emotions she was experiencing.

Did all women feel like this about the right man? The man who had the power to turn their universe upside down? It was a startling discovery that far from being the rather sexually cool person she had always considered herself she was capable of such deep and diverse needs. Just looking at him, studying the way his hair grew thick and dark into the nape of his neck made her shudder in sensual reaction her fingers already imagining the feel of his hair against them, the heavy thud of his heart against hers.

She started to tremble again and was startled by the sound of his voice as he stood up having unlocked the car, and opened the passenger door for her. 'Please get in. . . .'

The words were said with cool formality, but there was nothing cool nor formal about the way he was looking at her, and suddenly Sienna was reminded of her twenty-first birthday party and the way she had felt after consuming two glasses of champagne, only this time the bubbles of happiness really did seem to explode inside her. She shook her head slightly as she obeyed him and slid into the sleek interior of the waiting Mercedes, as though still half believing she was caught up in some fantasy daydream, but that notion was firmly dispelled when Alexis got in beside her, turning to her with a smile that set her pulses racing.

'The seat-belt mechanism is automatic,' he told her softly. 'Here, let me help you.'

He took the belt from her nerveless fingers, quickly slotting it into place, half leaning across her, her body intimately aware of the hard warmth of his, her eyes lifting from the deft, skilled movements of his fingers to the dark planes of his face. A faint stubble darkened his jaw, and her heart lurched spectacularly, her fingers itching to reach out and touch his skin, motivated by an irresistible urge to discover if his jaw felt as tough as it looked. Outwardly he bore all the trappings of wealth and sophistication; all the hallmarks of a man well used to the luxuries that money could buy, but it was the man within that drew Sienna; and she knew that wealthy or not he would still have drawn her in the same way, and not just her, she admitted on another lurching heartbeat; he possessed the sort of sexual magnetism that few women would be able to resist. Suddenly she wanted to know everything there was to know about him, and was close to tears to think of all the years when she hadn't known him; as a child; an adolescent; a young man, and she shivered fitfully, the tension in her body communicating itself to him as he completed his task and straightened up, his arm brushing briefly across her breasts.

The contact only lasted a matter of seconds, but it was long enough for Sienna to feel the immediate response of her body, and to gauge from Alexis' sudden tension and inheld breath that he was aware of it too. He turned towards her, his eyes resting on the soft swell of her body concealed by the fine wool of her jacket. His glance lifted to her face his eyes dark and hot, the desire she could feel surging inside herself mirrored in their depths, his attention drawn to linger again on the thrust of her breasts.

Her mouth was as dry as parchment, and Sienna knew that if he chose to he could make love to her here and now and she would glory in his possession of her womanhood. He turned, fastening his own seat-belt, his knuckles gleaming faintly through the tautness of his skin as he set the car in motion, and Sienna knew that there hadn't been a thought or emotion she had experienced since meeting him that he hadn't known of and shared.

The knowledge was so unfamiliar and so heady that she sat silent as he manoeuvred the large car through the heavy lunchtime traffic, sending up a mental prayer of gratitude to whoever it was who directed her fate that she had been permitted this glorious enchantment. It was awesome to think of the faint threads of chance from which so much human happiness dangled. If Alexis hadn't been recommended to try the agency; if she hadn't been there. . . .

'We're here.' His cool, faintly husky voice broke through her thoughts. A doorman opened the car door and she stepped out, vaguely aware of Alexis saying something to him and the crisp crackle of new notes, and then they were stepping into the foyer, and Alexis was directing her towards the lift, his lazy, long stride covering the thickly carpeted ground so quickly that she almost had to run to catch up with him.

He had a large suite at his disposal and someone had set up a desk with an expensive electronic typewriter and a small computer keyboard and VDU. There was another desk with three telephones and an in-tray stuffed full of papers. Sienna took most of it in in one single glance; after all, apart from the luxurious surroundings it was the sort of background she was now familiar with; the typewriter was a make she knew and had worked on before, and the computer presented no problems if she was required to use it. Mentally blessing Rob's forethought in insisting on sending her on a three-day computer course when she first arrived in London, she started to slide her coat from her shoulders, tensing when she felt Alexis' hands on her arms, his warm breath stirring the hair at the nape as he bent to assist her.

She was trembling and she couldn't stop; one part of her mind still bemused and half inclined to be appalled that she could feel like this; that she could be so ready to turn into his arms and let herself become part of him on such a short acquaintanceship, but the older, eternal womanly core of her urged her to follow her instincts to listen to what her heart was telling her and ignore the restrictions of generations of programming.

Suddenly she was fiercely glad that there had been no one else; no other touch to sully the pleasure she would find in Alexis' arms; a primaeval and intense need to give herself to this man and this man alone.

He removed her coat and hung it up on the stand by the door, while Sienna watched him, her body as attuned to his as the gazelle's to the hunter, quivering finely, every nerve ending aware of his presence and the frisson of pleasure it caused against her skin. When he returned to her he took her in his arms, simply holding her, looking down at her for several seconds, while Sienna returned his regard, knowing what he was reading in her face and eyes and making no attempt to hide her love and adoration from him.

'Tell me that it's true what your eyes are saying to me so eloquently; tell me that there's never been any man you've felt about the way you feel about me.' And then before she could respond his lips were brushing hers, lightly and then not so lightly as he felt her immediate response, her mouth parting eagerly, hungry for the hard possession of his.

If it was possible to become intoxicated by sheer happiness then that was what must have happened to her, Sienna thought dizzily as Alexis' lips left hers, travelling teasingly across her face; touching lightly against her fluttering eyelashes, closing her eyes, exploring the tender curve of her jaw; his fingers pushing aside her hair, his hands tightening their grip as he felt her involuntary response to the caress of his tongue and lips against her ear and the soft column of her throat, her body arching shamelessly against him as she responded with blind instinct to his touch.

At last his mouth returned to hers, touching, taking, possessing. Her hands slid under his jacket and found the hard muscles of his back, her body glorying in the sudden aroused tension of his; in the way he held her against him, his hands moving down to her thighs, pressing her into his body, and then slowly releasing her as he ended the kiss. He took a step away from her and smiled down into her flushed, bemused face, his thumb softly probing the mouth his had just bruised with such devastating hunger. 'So . . .' he said softly, 'it has begun. . . .'

'You . . . you felt it too?' Sienna asked hesitantly, groping for the right words to describe her feelings and aware that those she had chosen were hopelessly inadequate to describe them. Two hours ago she hadn't known that he existed, and now . . . now she was so deeply in love with him that nothing else mattered but him.

'I felt it too,' he confirmed, still keeping that small, tantalising distance between them. 'Together we will make the world rock and feel its hushed tremble, my little virgin. When I make love to you and my body finally possesses yours it will be as though we are immortals, gods, and not mere human beings, but as yet you know nothing of the pleasure that will be ours. No other man has shown you what I shall show you. I shall be the first.'

He said it with such assurance that she held her breath, staring wonderingly into his face. It was as though he had always known her; as though he knew everything there was to know about her, and so all she did was murmur slowly, 'and the last. . . .' And then watched his eyes darken, with the same kind of wonder and awe with which she had listened to carols being sung on Christmas Eve as a child, the lump in her throat threatening to render her completely speechless. Alexis saw her reaction and laughed deep in his throat, a husky, satisfied sound, and she knew that the fact that she was still a virgin was pleasing him.

'Ah, yes, we shall be lovers, you and I,' he promised her, 'but not today ... not yet. First we shall enjoy the anticipation a little, and I shall try to school myself to playing the suitor rather than the lover. Also there is work to do, because I wasn't lying about my need for a secretary.'

Work? After this? Sienna stared mutely at him, but as she discovered as the day progressed he hadn't been joking. Marvelling at his ability to change from lover to employer, she tried to follow his lead and concentrate on the detailed dictation he was giving her, all the time acutely conscious of the maleness of him; the way his trousers moulded the strong muscles of his thighs; the breadth of his shoulders and the depth of his chest in the clinging silk shirt that seemed to mould itself to his body.

In that afternon Sienna gained a brief understanding of how diverse his business interests were: he wasn't just the Chairman of Hellas Holidays, he also had an interest in an international airline, in villas on the islands, which he owned and let out, in olive groves, and even a vineyard in the Napa Valley in California. That had come to him through his mother, who Sienna deduced from the brief comments that he made had been half Italian and half American, which no doubt accounted for his height, and less swarthy complexion than she might have expected. It also explained the grey eyes which were so totally unexpected and devasting in the pure symmetry of a face which had its beginnings in the very best of the ancient sculptures.

They worked without pause until six o'clock. Sienna felt limp and drained when they had finished. Alexis had dictated consistently in English, but she had translations to make into French and German, and she was relieved when he told her that she would have the best part of the following morning to work on what he had just given her.

'I shall be in meetings for most of the morning.' He saw her face and smiled, and the dying rays of the sun streaming through the windows lingered against his skin casting shadows that gave him a faintly cynical, predatory air, and one which was totally at odds with the man Sienna thought him to be. She shivered in spite of herself, faintly repelled by the transformation, the cold, almost detached air with which he seemed to be studying her, but then he moved and it was gone, and she laughed inwardly at her own folly. It had been a trick of the sunlight, nothing more, and she forgot that he was a man who came from a land that was more used to harsh sunlight then gentle shadows, she forgot everything as he came towards her, pulling her out of her chair, gently removing her pad and pencil from nerveless fingers, framing her face with his hands as he studied her wildly flushed features.

'Tomorrow I must work, but we still have tonight. Will you let me take you out to dinner?'

Would she? Sienna moistened her lips and trembled as she saw the flaring reaction of his eyes to the gesture and felt its echo in his body.

'No, I am not going to take you to my bed tonight,' he muttered accurately reading her mind . . . 'but one night, not so very far from now when you are ready for me, I shall.'

I'm ready now, Sienna wanted to tell him, half appalled by her own immodesty and hunger, but he was already releasing her, putting her away from him, smiling at her as he asked politely, 'Will you be able to be ready by half past eight? I'll book a table for nine. Aristotle, my chauffeur, is waiting downstairs to take you home. Unfortunately I am expecting an important call from New York, otherwise I would go with you. Do you live alone?'

With a shock Sienna realised it was the first personal question he had asked her. Somehow exchanging past histories had seemed irrelevant, but now she managed to murmur, 'No . . . with my brother, but he's away at the moment. He's a reporter. Our parents are dead, and Rob very kindly took me in when our father died. I used to work for him, you see, and when he died I just didn't know what to do with myself.'

'You love your brother very deeply?'

Sienna frowned, wondering at the darkness in his eyes and the curt iciness in his voice. Surely he wasn't jealous of Rob? 'Yes,' she replied simply. 'Everyone likes him. He's a marvellous person, so kind and thoughtful. . . .'

'And he has a woman, this kind and thoughtful brother?'

Sienna hesitated, disturbed by the thread of sarcasm she could sense woven into the words. 'I . . . I don't know,' she finished lamely, feeling it would be wrong to discuss her suspicions about Rob's feelings for Gillian with anyone else, even Alexis.

'So. . . . Then he has never discussed with you a special woman, this wonderful brother of yours whom you so admire?'

He *must* be jealous, Sienna thought blankly, there could be no other reason for the dislike and, yes, almost hatred embittering his voice. 'Never,' she responded resolutely.

'You had better leave now, Aristotle will be waiting.' The abrupt change of subject startled her a little at first, but Sienna accepted it, thinking there would be time that evening to question Alexis about his family and background.

She went over to the door and shrugged into her coat, picking up her bag. 'And, Sienna . . .' She paused, wondering if he was going to change his mind and command her to remain with him after all. He smiled, warmth infusing the darkness of his features and making her weak with the need to go to him and touch him. 'Yes?'

'Tonight wear something that permits me to see a little more of your body than the clothes you are wearing now. That way I shall have something to warm my lonely bed tonight.'

He saw her face and shook his head. 'No, this is no brief casual thing between us, and I will not hurry it. When a man finds the food which is to last him for the rest of his life he does not consume it with greed as though it were his final feast. Now go,' he said softly, 'before I forget all my lofty ideals and remember only how badly I want to make you mine.'

All the way down in the lift her heart sang. Alexis had put the final seal on her happiness. He wanted her, not just for now, but for always, it had been implicit in his final words to her. She thought of having Alexis as her husband, of bearing his children, and her body shook with the pleasure the thought gave her.

CHAPTER TWO

As she dressed for her dinner date with Alexis, Sienna found herself going over and over in her mind the circumstances of their meeting; re-living the touch of his hands against her face and the warm, intoxicating pressure of his mouth on hers. It took her half an hour to decide what to wear, delicious tremors shivering across her skin as she remembered his parting words. In the end she opted for a dress she had bought when she had to accompany her father to a dance at the university.

Far more sophisticated than the clothes she usually chose, it was in matt black jersey, cut to reveal the svelte contours of her body, outwardly demure with its high rounded neckline and long close-fitting sleeves, but the way it moulded her body was far from demure. Would Alexis find her attractive in it? It was startling to discover how much she wanted to be alluring for him; in the past she had always been careful to dress in clothes that masked her sexuality rather than revealed it and had even been faintly scornful of those women she knew who dressed mainly to please their men. It was a strange and almost frightening sensation to have fallen so deeply in love so quickly, and Sienna knew that if Alexis hadn't made it so clear to her that her feelings were reciprocated she would be maintaining as great a distance as she possibly could from him. For the first time in her life she could imagine the desolation of unrequited love; it shivered across her skin chilly as a

November wind, until she pulled the reassuring, warming blanket of Alexis' love back round her.

He arrived to pick her up himself, and her breath caught in her throat as she studied him beneath the hall light. 'Your heart quivers like a frightened dove's. What is it that frightens you so? Surely not me?' His fingers curled round her wrist, his thumb probing for and then stroking the swiftly beating pulse.

How could she explain that the reality of him far exceeded the mental picture she had carried away with her, that falling in love with him was something so totally outside any experience she had ever expected to have that it left her weak and, yes, slightly frightened by the knowledge of her new vulnerability. Yesterday she hadn't known he existed; today her life would be insupportable without him. He seemed to know what she was thinking, because he lifted her wrist to his lips, their heat sending waves of pleasure beating through her veins, his eyes hot and slumbrous with desire as they slid slowly over her face and body.

'It *is* frightening. I have felt it too,' he assured her. 'To be so dependent on another person for happiness—for life itself.'

'And you've never felt like this before?' He was thirty-three, Gill had told her that, and his name had been linked with those of many, many beautiful women. It seemed to Sienna incredible that he could feel this way about her.

'I have never felt towards any woman what I feel towards you.' The words had the unmistakable ring of sincerity. She trembled beneath them, the hallway suddenly cramped and infused with the same subtle tension she had sensed the first time she saw him. 'Ah, Sienna, you must not look at me like that. How can you look at me the way you do and still have remained a virgin? Your eyes tell me that you want me to make love to you.'

'I do.' She whispered the words shyly, still amazed that she could feel this way, that there could be this depth and intensity of feeling, something she had never suspected existed. 'And I am still a virgin because I have never looked at any other man the way I look at you. I have never loved any man before you. . . .'

'And will not love any man after me. I shall imprint myself on your heart and body so that you will never forget me. We have not yet made love, but already I know how you will feel in my arms, how you will taste against my lips, how sweetly you will cry my name and abandon yourself to me.'

He bent his head, sliding his fingers into the thickness of her hair, holding her still beneath his mouth, letting her feel the depth and heat of his passion, leaving her shaking and achingly bereft when he eventually lifted his head, his lips curling into a smile as he caught her half-smothered protest.

'So reserved and English,' he murmured, probing the parted warmth of her mouth with his thumb, 'but I promise you I will make you forget your reserve and the politeness of your good manners, and in my arms will remember only that you are a woman.' He smiled down at her, a dark seriousness in his eyes that stilled the frantic racing of her pulses. 'I cannot promise you that I will be a tender, gentle lover, Sienna, my need for you does not permit that. If you wish to change your mind, to retreat, then now is the time to do so, while I am still able to let you go.'

He knew! He knew how fear mingled with her love for him, how tremulous she felt about committing herself completely to him, about walking blindfold into waters which she sensed were deep and dangerous and he was offering her the chance to turn back. She returned his smile with one of her own faintly wavering and hesitant, unaware of the shy vulnerability glowing in her eyes as they met his.

'I don't want to turn back, Alexis,' she told him huskily. 'I fell in love with you the moment you walked into Gill's office. I. . . .' She tried to find the words to describe the awe and wonder of that moment, then gave up, knowing that it was a feat beyond her.

'And if I had not fallen in love with you in return?'

She shivered, despite the warmth of Rob's centrally heated flat. 'I don't know. . . .' How could she explain to him that she wasn't the type of girl who had the confidence to go out and get the man she wanted, that if she hadn't seen the desire, the hunger in his eyes she would have had to dam up her feelings for him?

'Your silence is its own answer,' Alexis told her. 'Without the security of my admission of love you would never have been able to bring yourself to tell me of your feelings. You would have worked for me as my temporary secretary, harbouring impossible dreams, is this is not so?'

It startled her a little that he should so accurately be able to judge her reactions, for that was exactly how she would have behaved, envying the women who shared his life, but totally unable to emulate them.

'Do not look so chastened.' His hand caressed

her jaw, tilting her face so that he could look into her eyes. 'I knew the moment I opened the office door how it would be between us, and because you are what you are, the only place I shall hold you in my arms tonight is on the dance floor. I want you to come to me willingly, Sienna—more than willingly,' he added huskily, 'knowingly, wantingly, as hungry for me as I am for you.'

She wanted to tell him then that that was already how she felt about him, but because he was right when he said that she was still a little shy and uncertain of herself, she allowed him to escort her to the waiting car, and half an hour later when they were seated at their table in a fashionable nightclub she had only read about in the Society columns, she no longer regretted her silence.

Her arrival with Alexis had caused something of a stir. Heads had turned, and Sienna knew quite well that they had not turned on her behalf. Several eager pairs of female eyes followed their progress to their table. How many of the women dining here with other men were known to Alexis? she wondered as she sat down, and not just here in London, but in all those other cities where he had business interests and offices. It shook her to feel so vulnerable and, yes, jealous. Alexis was nine years older than her and what was past was past.

'Is something troubling you?' He leaned across the table, attentive and concerned, and she pushed away her dark thoughts, a little saddened by the knowledge that love brought pain as well as pleasure.

She asked him to order for her. Although she was perfectly used to dining out both with her father and Rob, neither of them had ever taken her to such an openly luxurious place. Most of the other women were wearing rich jewels and couture gowns, and even though she knew it was foolish, Sienna was aware of feeing slightly ill at ease.

The food Alexis chose was delicious, but she discovered that she had little appetite for it. She was too aware of the man seated opposite her, of the movement of his body beneath the covering of expensive clothes, of the lean darkness of his hands, her mind unable to stop picturing them on her body, causing a heated flush to rise up over her skin, and Alexis to break off from what he had been saying, to ask with a frown, 'Sienna, are you all right?'

'Yes. . . .' She sounded flustered. 'It's . . . it's very warm in here, isn't it?'

'Is it?' His eyes narrowed in perceptive amusement. 'I confess I hadn't noticed it. Would you like to dance?'

She glanced at the small dimly lit dance floor and then back again to Alexis' darkly masculine face. There was nowhere she wanted to be more than in his arms, and her eyes must have given her away, because he muttered something thickly under his breath and put down the glass he had been holding, with fingers that were distinctly unsteady, his hoarse, 'Yes . . . yes, I know, but I will not take you in hungry greed, however much both of us want to at this moment, and since I cannot make love to you on the dance floor, we are safer there than sitting here, where your eyes tell me with every breath you draw what you are thinking and my body responds to that knowledge.'

Alexis had lied when he said he couldn't make love to her on the dance floor, Sienna thought minutes later; the firm movement of his thighs against hers turning her bones to water, making her grateful for the dimness of the lights and the seductive tempo of the music which enabled them to move so slowly together, her body registering every movement of Alexis'. She could feel his heart thudding beneath the hand she had slipped inside his jacket. Both his arms were round her, pressing her against him, caressing the vulnerable arc of her spine, his lips feathering, brief, tormenting kisses against her temple.

'You tremble so in my arms,' Alexis murmured against her ear. 'It makes me ache to possess you, do you know that?' He felt her body's response and his own hardened against her, his chest expanding as he dragged air into his lungs. 'No, you don't know yet what you do to me, how you make me burn and shake with need, but I will teach you, Sienna.'

Teach me now, she wanted to cry out, but the tempo of the music changed and with it the mood he had created around them. In a daze she allowed him to lead her back to their table. They must have talked, but later she could remember nothing of what they had said. All she could think of when she lay alone in her bed in Rob's flat was that Alexis had wanted her and that for her sake he had denied himself because he didn't want to rush her. Had denied them both, she acknowledged feverishly, understanding now the deep-seated ache that lay curled in the pit of her stomach, sending stabbing waves of need coursing through the rest of her body. Her total turn-around from a cool, remote young woman to this hungry aching feline creature who now seemed to live inside her skin took some getting used to, and as she lay wanting Alexis she wondered on a sudden dark presentiment if this new part of herself might not have been better left undiscovered.

By morning she had forgotten her night fears, her fingers clumsy in her feverish haste to dress and reach Alexis. She glanced at herself in the mirror, noting the changes that were there already; the flush high along her cheekbones, the brightness of her eyes, one minute sparkling, the next disconcertingly slumbrous. Excitement made it impossible for her to eat, to do anything more than snatch a cup of coffee as she hurried to get ready.

Alexis was waiting for her in his suite, studying a pile of letters. He looked up when she walked in but made no move to touch her. 'I'm just about to leave.' He smiled wryly when he saw her face and added softly, 'Ah, no, I must not kiss you, otherwise I shall never make it to my meetings—never make it any further than the bedroom that lies beyond that door, but tomorrow is Saturday. Would you like to go for a drive? To have lunch somewhere perhaps, and then in the evening we could see a show?'

All I want to do is to be with you, she ached to tell him, but instead she followed the lead he had given her, assuring him that she ought to have finished the dictation he had given her the previous day by the time he got back and that she could find no fault in his plans for the following day.

And so it continued. During the day they worked together in comparative harmony. Sienna grew gradually to learn more about his business empire and to admire his shrewd grasp of all that went on within it, even though at times his hard

determination had the power to disturb her. That
he could be cruel as Gill had said he was she
could now perceive was true, and she shivered
sometimes, wondering what she would do if that
cruelty was ever directed towards her. At those
times he would look up from what he was doing
and smile at her as though he guessed her thoughts
and wanted to assure her that her fears were
groundless.

He often asked her about Rob, and when he did
Sienna sensed as she had done on that first day
that he resented—and if that could be possible
without their having met—even disliked her
brother, but when she tried to question him about
his own family he always changed the subject.

A week and then ten days went by. She arrived
one morning to discover him on the telephone.
'New York,' he said crisply when he replaced the
receiver. 'I have to go over there—there's a
problem with the merger.'

Sienna knew that one of his companies was
taking over an American rival, but her face fell
when Alexis was speaking.

'How long . . . how long will you be gone?' How
long will you be away from me, was what she
really wanted to know, and yet how long would he
be staying in London for anyway? His home was
in Greece, on a small island called Micros, he had
told her. He had talked about it to her, with love
and pride and an assurance that she would share it
with him.

'I don't know. Three weeks, maybe a month. It
will take that long to sort out all the legal tangles.'
He saw her expression and muttered huskily,
'Sienna, don't. You know I don't want to leave
you, and we still have this weekend. Would you

like to go away somewhere. ... Just the two of us?'

'Oh, Alexis!' Her eyes and voice betrayed her, and he did something he never did when they were working, he got up from his chair and crossed the room, taking her in his arms and kissing her with the same deep hunger she could feel heating her own blood.

'Does that mean "yes"? You know if it does that I shall not be able to kiss you chastely goodnight and leave you, Sienna. You know, don't you,' he asked roughly, 'that when you say "yes", you are saying yes to sharing my bed? Do you still say "yes"?'

She shook her head and he tensed, holding her away from him and staring down at her with dark, almost angry eyes, and Sienna knew that despite all his protestations he wanted her enough to persuade her if she did not agree voluntarily. Not that there was any need. She wanted this weekend with him, needed it with an urgency that still had the power to leave her slightly shocked. 'Then what do you say?' he demanded curtly.

She smiled up at him, feeling the tension in the arms that held her, a brief smile curling her mouth as she said softly, 'I say "yes, please", Alexis.'

She felt the surge of tension leaving him, and just had time to be surprised by the look of sheer triumph glittering in his eyes as he bent towards her, kissing her more gently this time, merging her body with his, his fingers tangling in her hair as he released her lips to caress the soft skin of her throat, his fingers deftly moving to the buttons of her blouse, releasing them and exposing the pulse thudding at the base of her neck and the beginnings of the soft swell of her breasts, her nipples tautly outlined beneath the fine cotton of her blouse.

Strange, he had not yet touched her intimately, but when he did so, pushing aside the protection of her blouse, stroking over the curves her delicate lace bra did nothing to conceal, her body leapt in immediate response, her low groan of pleasure stifled somewhere at the back of her throat as his head moved downwards and she gasped as she felt the heat and dampness of his mouth through the fine fabric, coupled with an anguished ache to lie naked in his arms and enjoy that same caress with the barrier of clothes removed. The phone rang, disorientating her, her body still awash with hunger. Her mind was too bemused to respond to the abrupt summons of the telephone. Alexis answered it, frowning into the receiver, reminding Sienna where they were. She dressed quickly, with shaking fingers, wondering heatedly what her reaction was likely to be to his full possession if she could be affected so much by a mere caress. She was still lost in a maze of thoughts when he replaced the receiver and came to stand behind her.

'You look like a child who has suddenly discovered Christmas,' he told her with amusement, obviously relishing her embarrassment. 'What a contradiction you are! Outwardly so cool and calm, and inwardly so responsively sensual, and I only have to look at you and I see mirrored in your eyes what will be there when I make love to you. I cannot believe no man has make you feel like this before. Has there, Sienna? Has there been a man who has made the earth shake for you, a man with whom you have shared desire?'

She shook her head and watched his eyes lighten

with relief, and wondered if he knew what joy it gave her that he should be the first, that she had waited for the magic of giving herself to him and sharing with him her body's arousal from innocence to desire.

'I am going to take you away somewhere where no one will disturb us, where we will be completely alone, where when I want to kiss and touch you I can do so and know that we won't be interrupted.' He kissed her briefly then, his mouth hard and warm and the same delirious drunken feeling of disbelief she had experienced on first seeing him surged giddily through her again. 'You love me?'

'So much,' she told him huskily, 'So very, very much!'

When she got home there was a letter from Rob telling her that his return was likely to be delayed and that it could be several more weeks before he returned. She was disappointed. She would have liked Alexis to meet him before he went to New York. She wanted Alexis to understand why she loved him and why that love was no threat to the way he felt about her, but she didn't want to spoil their weekend together, so she firmly banished her disappointment and concentrated on what she ought to pack.

Alexis hadn't told her where they were going apart from the fact that it was in the country and they would be completely alone, and she packed accordingly, jeans and sweaters, one simple dress that would cover eating out, a soft tweed suit to travel in and . . . she tried not to feel guilty as she added up the cost of the expensive, delicate underwear she had bought on impulse on her way home the previous evening. She had paused outside the shop, admiring as she always did its elegant window, staring at the costly wisps of silk and lace, knowing how far they were outside her reach and yet wanting Alexis to see her dressed in something so essentially feminine, knowing instinctively that such a very male man would find pleasure in the knowledge that it was worn only for him.

And so she had gone in, and come out again half an hour later, carrying the boxes whose contents she was now carefully packing into her case. The silk chiffon nightdress was soft pale peach trimmed with écru lace, handmade and delicate as cobwebs. The underwear she was wearing to travel in was cream silk-satin, and her fingers smoothed it absently as she tried to still the quiver of excitement starting deep inside her.

She was ready and too excited to finish her breakfast, half an hour before Alexis was due to arrive. Incredible to think that this was actually her and that tonight she would sleep in Alexis' arms, his body next to hers. As always when she thought about touching him, about him making love to her, she was overwhelmed by her reaction to her thoughts. And she wasn't going to allow herself to think beyond the weekend to the empty weeks when he would be in New York, and she would be here, or about how she was going to endure their separation.

'We'll soon be stopping for lunch. Are you hungry?' Only for him, Sienna thought nervously, turning in her seat to give him a brief smile and shaking her head. Why this sense of nervousness and anxiety now when this was what she had wanted from the very moment she first saw him, for them to be together?

They were almost in the New Forest; their

destination, so Alexis had informed her when he picked her up. He had rented a small cottage for them for the weekend, but first they were to have lunch at a hotel which had been recommended to him.

'It used to be a private house,' he told her as he turned into the driveway. They specialise in Nouvelle Cuisine.'

She might as well have been served with the unappetising stodge she remembered from school lunches, Sienna thought guiltily an hour and half later, watching Alexis cut himself a wedge of Stilton. She could watch his hands for ever, they were so very beautiful in a totally male way, lean and brown, his fingers long and filbert-nailed, every movement they made deft and precise and yet somehow sensual, as though they knew secrets which were as yet unknown to her. She had refused a sweet, too full of the tension which had been with her ever since they set out. She was being ridiculous, she chided herself mentally, acting like a teenager who didn't know the first thing about sex, her movements jerky, her whole body betraying her apprehension, and yet this was what she wanted. If Alexis were to announce that he had changed his mind and they were going back to London she would be bitterly, achingly disappointed.

She glanced quickly up at him. His features were impassive, relaxed, and yet she was aware of something elemental that sent shivers of alarm tingling along her spine. Was it because of her innocence that she felt like this, her ignorance and näiveté, or was it because of his male aura, because of the hunter she sensed lurking beneath the svelte layers of civilisation? This was a man whose heritage was Greek; a man born of a country that put a high price on its women's virtue, a country where a man could and still did expect to marry a virgin bride. Would she be devaluing herself in his eyes by giving herself to him like this, would he in spite of his claims to love her despise her afterwards?

Where had such dark thoughts sprung from? Hadn't she always despised women who bartered their bodies for the security of a wedding ring? She loved Alexis, and he loved her, he had told her so. So where had this feeling of insecurity come from? Perhaps the fact that he must leave her? But he would return, he had told her so, he had talked about their future together. . . .

'Having second thoughts?' How easily he read her mind, startling her by voicing thoughts she had believed to be secret.

'Sort of.' Her eyes pleaded with him for reassurance.

'And you want me to persuade you into bed with me?' He stood up, shaking his head, his breath brushing her ear as he leaned forward and murmured softly, 'No, Sienna, I won't do it. You must come to me of your own free will. You must give of yourself freely, or not at all.' He moved back and she could see how his eyes had changed from light to dark with the intensity of his feelings. Tears clogged in her throat. How could she have doubted him? How could she have harboured such thoughts about a man who said openly that he would not put any pressure on her?

'Well?' He was guiding her out of the hotel, to where his car waited. 'Have you changed your mind? Do you want to return to London and your virginal bed?'

The warmth of his arm felt so right against her waist, his hip hard against her softness, and she raised her face to him shaking her head. 'No.' Her voice was husky, tremulous with all that she felt and could not say. 'No, Alexis, I want to go on.'

He smiled and in that smile she saw all his male triumph, all his pleasure in her admission, and yet she could not begrudge it to him. As he opened her car door for her he bent towards her, brushing the softness of her lips with the hardness of his own. 'You can't know how much it means to me to hear you say that, Sienna ... but later ... tonight, I will show you.'

The cottage was perfect, remote, surrounded by the sounds of the forest, intimate and cosily furnished so that she felt at home the moment she stepped down into the small living room and felt its warmth enclose her.

There was a kitchen, beautifully fitted out with warm oak units, a meal had been left prepared for them and merely needed heating up. Although the cottage was centrally heated it was cool enough for her to be tempted when Alexis offered to light the open fire in the living room. The ceiling of the room was so low that when he stood upright his head barely scraped under the ancient beams.

'I'll see to the fire while you unpack,' he told her, getting down on his knees, his back to her. She was sure he had done it deliberately, sensing the panic that had been building up inside her at the thought of going up those narrow stairs with him behind her. The cottage only possessed one bedroom, prettily decorated by someone with a liking for Laura Ashley, and the bathroom adjacent was decorated to match. The room felt warm and homely, so much more intimate than a hotel would have been.

The perfect place for a honeymoon, Sienna thought yearningly, then caught back the thought. She was being so silly behaving like this as though she were the victim of some seduction plan and about to be transformed into a scarlet woman! She was free to leave even now if she wanted to. She was here with Alexis because she wanted to be. She dawdled over unpacking what little she had brought with her. There was no need for her to change, the suit she had travelled down in was a soft heather tweed and was perfectly suitable for spending the evening in.

'Fire's lit. Do you fancy a drink?' Alexis' voice, so calm, calmed her frenzied nerves, his mundane question taking her to the head of the stairs to give an assent. 'While you're up there will you unpack for me?'

Ridiculous to feel so embarrassed about touching his clothes. How many times had she packed for Rob or her father and never given it another thought, but these things belonged to the man who would soon be her lover, and it was different. She noticed that he hadn't packed any pyjamas, and felt her skin flush even though there was no one there to see it, or to witness the way her eyes darkened at the thought of his body against hers. She felt as though she knew him already, but she didn't and she hurried over her task, anxious to return downstairs and reassure herself that the whole thing wasn't just a dream.

'Tired?'

The Beethoven had come to a close, and there was really nothing to keep them downstairs any longer. The fire had burned down and Alexis' glass was empty. They had finished dinner three hours ago, and now as she listened to the dying crackle of the last apple log Sienna lifted her head from his shoulder.

'Mmm . . . a little. . . .' She felt the laughter shake his body and tensed, feeling childishly hurt. He must have done this so many times before, while she. . . .

'Ah, no, you are wrong.' Again he had read her mind and he turned to her in the light from the fire, cupping her face with his hands, his eyes sombre, brooding almost, reminding her of that ancient heritage she had seen in him earlier. 'There have been other times, but none before like this . . . none that have meant as much to me as this does. I shall ask you again, Sienna, do you come to me willingly? Do you?'

'Yes . . . yes!' She said it fiercely, pushing back all her doubts and fears, willing him to help her to sweep them away with the magic of his touch. His mouth brushed hers, gently, slowly, his thumb probing the softness of her lips until they parted and his tongue ran lightly over the fullness of her lower one. Her breath caught in the back of her throat, the faintest sound, but he heard it and responded to it, his hand sliding along her throat, tangling in the thickness of her hair, bending her head back against his arm, the hunger building in him as his mouth closed on hers.

She was melting, dissolving, turning into something that wasn't flesh and bone, but just feeling, under the heat of his kiss. She was drowning in her response to him, lost beneath the fiery trail of kisses that tormented her skin, shivering beneath a need so great that she was deaf, dumb and blind to anything else.

'Sienna.... Tell me you love me.... You *do* love me, don't you?' The words were punctuated with kisses that turned her mindless with frenzied hunger, the feel of his hands on her body beneath the silk of her blouse making her arch and mutter his name.

'Totally, completely,' she told him breathlessly, responding to the demand of his questions, shivering beneath his touch.

'Ah, I do not think you have done even this many times before, have you?' His fingers stroked the racing pulses under her skin, his mouth suddenly gentle.

'Never,' Sienna told him.

'Never?' His eyes darkened with openly perceptible arousal. 'How innocently you say the word, not knowing that you are offering me the most potent form of temptation I have ever endured! Do you really not know what it does to me to know that I shall be the first to teach you the meaning of desire, to see passion blaze in your eyes....'

'You have already taught me,' Sienna told him shakily, and she was lost amidst billowing clouds of pleasure as he laughed and said softly, 'You think this is pleasure? You have much to learn, and suddenly I am in a very great hurry to teach you.'

He picked her up, carrying her as lightly as though she weighed nothing, her face buried against the warmth of his shoulder, the scent of his skin filling her senses.

He placed her on the bed, leaning over her, smiling down at her. 'How you tremble in my arms—with willingness or with fear, my sweet virgin?'

'Both,' Sienna admitted honestly, 'but willingness overrides fear. . . .'

'As desire shall override both,' he promised her. 'I do not want you as a sacrifice, not matter how willing, but as an eager participant, as a woman who wants a man—the man! How you tremble still,' he muttered, feeling her response to his words, and bent his head to place his lips against the warm hollow between her breasts, his fingers deft on the remaining buttons of her blouse. Against the fine silk of her camisole the burgeoning arousal of her nipples was clearly discernible. 'But there is nothing to fear but fear, and for the brave the ultimate reward is unquantifiable; there is no price, no limit, no standard that can be placed on the pleasure of giving and receiving love'.

Through the thin silk his thumb probed the thrusting outline of her nipple and fierce pleasure throbbed through her, burning in a hot tide as he slid the silk away and brushed the dark aureole of flesh with his tongue, circling and stroking until she clutched mindlessly at his shoulders, gasping his name and shivering with the awareness of all that passion could be and the paucity of her ability to imagine what it might have been beforehand.

Hours, or was it only minutes later, she really didn't know because time seemed to be suspended, Alexis was guiding her hands against his body, smiling at her wide-eyed awe at its beauty, as unembarrassed at his nudity as she was shy of hers, his mouth slightly skimming her skin, teasing, tantalising, arousing until she forgot all her anxiety about what she did not know and remembered only that he was the man she loved and that his skin tasted warm and salt against her lips and that her touch had the power to make him tense and shudder as vulnerable to her as she was to him.

His hands framed her face, his mouth hot on hers, compelling her response, sweeping her into the fierce surge of pleasure swirling through her body, the full powerful weight of him against her, the tension uncoiling from her body and a deep aching need taking its place.

She needed no urging to return his caresses when his hands and mouth roved over her body, inciting it to arch and echo the soft pleas mixed with the kisses she scattered against his skin. A voice inside her cried out that this was what she had been made for, and not even the powerful thrust of his body against hers had the power to frighten her.

'Do you love me?' He murmured the words against her mouth, moulding her hips with his hands, and then sliding them beneath her as he felt her body's rhythmic response, and her moaned 'Yes . . . Yes. . . .'

His mouth brushed hers again as he lifted her towards him, parting her thighs with his, rasping the softness of her flesh. 'Then give yourself to me,' he demanded hoarsely. 'All of you, Sienna . . . I want it all.'

The words echoed and resounded through her body and it responded elementally to them, welcoming his penetration, and then recoiling from the pain of it, more intense than she had dreamed possible. Alexis' curse reaching her from far away, the surging pressure of his possession of her now something alien and to be feared rather than welcomed.

She lay beneath him, still trembling, trying

valiantly to remember how much she had wanted him and trying equally valiantly to squash her pain and disillusionment and her fear that after all she had been right and she was not a woman who was ever going to experience great physical pleasure.

'Did I hurt you?' He sounded cold, distant, angry almost, and something inside her tensed as he moved away from her. Had she disappointed him? She must have done after all the women he had known. . . .

'A little,' she lied, 'but it will be better . . . next time. . . .' Her eyes pleaded with him for confirmation, for the words of reassurance and love to bring balm to her aching body, but he was standing up, shrugging the broad shoulders she had so recently worshipped with her lips, his expression bored and cynical.

'No doubt it will,' he agreed, 'but not with me, Sienna. You will have to find another lover to teach you pleasure.'

She couldn't take it in at first. She simply stared at him while the words played over and over in her numbed brain. 'You mean. . . .'

She tried to formulate her thoughts, but he cut across her husky, whisper and said curtly, 'What I mean is that I have achieved what I set out to do, and I have taken your viginity just as your brother took my sister's, but with a little more grace. *She* was brutally raped!'

'Raped!' Sienna struggled valiantly to make sense out of what he was saying, unable to comprehend what was happening; where the man she had believed to be her lover had gone, and who this stranger who had taken his place was. 'But you said you loved me . . . you. . . .'

'So naïve! Didn't your mother ever warn you

that that's what all men tell you when they want you go to bed with them? You were so easy to deceive,' he told her cruelly. 'Almost too easy.'

Sienna stole a glance at his dark, taunting face, her eyes drawn with a compulsion it was impossible for her to master to the cold clear outline of his mouth. Sickness and self-contempt welled up inside her. Dear God, what a fool she had been! He was right, she *had* made it easy for him, easy to steal her heart and destroy her precious daydreams with his words of love which had been nothing more than cruel lies.

'Drink this.' A glass of water was thrust in front of her, the liquid faintly cloudy. 'You should be thankful that I didn't take you as your brother did my sister; brutally, despoiling her. . . .'

'Rob wouldn't do that—I know he wouldn't! I think I hate you!' she added vehemently, her voice low and shaken.

'Hate me?' His mouth was wry 'Not half an hour ago you were telling me how much you loved me, that I and I alone held your heart. Sleep now. In the morning. . . .'

In the morning? Did he honestly expect her to stay here with him after what he had just said to her? Shock had robbed her of the ability to feel real pain, but she knew it was there waiting for her and when it began she wanted to be alone. She loved *him*, and *he* had just been using her, callously and completely without regard for her feelings. She had loved in ideal, she told herself fiercely, a dream image of a man who didn't exist. She must *not* love him, she must force herself to face the truth.

'I want to leave now,' she said curtly. 'I'll ring for a taxi.' She saw the surprise he couldn't quite conceal and said bitterly, 'What did you expect? That I would plead with you? Break down and *beg* you to love me? I've already made a fool of myself once tonight!'

'Sienna.' Incredibly he dared to touch her, frowning when she froze beneath the touch of his fingers on her arm. 'You must understand that I meant you no personal harm. . . .'

'No, I was just the means by which you accomplished your revenge,' she agreed tightly. 'What would you have done if Rob hadn't had a sister? If I *hadn't* been a virgin? How would you have played God then?'

She had the satisfaction of seeing his face darken in suppressed anger. 'I made it my business to find out everything I could about your brother and his family. Had you not existed I would have found another way, but this was the most fitting.'

'An eye for an eye,' Sienna agreed curtly. Was she really having this conversation? She felt as though she had strayed into some horrendous nightmare and only the terrible fear that she might break down and cry out her pain and anguish in front of this man—her enemy, enabled her to maintain control of her emotions.

'Where are you going?' he demanded as she reached for a robe—*his*, she noticed idly, and swung her feet to the floor.

'To ring for a taxi.'

His mouth compressed. 'We will leave in the morning. You needn't worry that I shall. . . .'

'Make love to me?' she threw back. 'I'm not. After all you achieved your purpose, didn't you, although I suppose as you've paid for the cottage for the weekend you might feel you want to get your money's worth. Well, I'm sure it won't be too

difficult for you to find someone else to share your
bed; a man of your wealth and talent. . . .' Her
mouth curled in bitter cynicism over the last words
and she saw the dark colour stain his high
cheekbones.

'Not difficult at all,' he agreed, taunting her,
'although they might not quite match *you* for
willingness. You wanted me to make love to you.'

'I wanted the man I stupidly thought you to be
to make love to me,' Sienna corrected, pulling on
his robe and walking towards the door. When he
made to follow her she turned on him, her eyes
blazing in the pale triangle of her face.

'Don't touch me! Don't come anywhere near
me. I can't stand the thought of you near me. Just
to be in the same room with you makes me feel
physically sick!' It wasn't a lie. She did feel sick,
but it didn't stop him coming towards her,
gripping her forearms and shaking her quite hard.

'Stop this! If you must leave now I'll drive you.'

'No!'

'Yes. Do you think I wanted to do this?' His
eyes were bleak. 'I promise you I had no
alternative. Sofia was betrothed, when your
brother raped her, to a cousin of ours, a young
man she had known since childhood. Of course he
had to be told the truth and the betrothal was
broken. Can you imagine what that did to her?
For a while we feared for her very sanity. For
Sofia's sake, I had to exact retribution. If you
want to find someone to blame, blame your
brother. . . .'

'No!' Sienna looked at him with all the
bitterness of her feelings in her eyes. 'No, I blame
myself for being stupid enough to believe that you
were capable of caring for me. Gill warned me that

you were cruel, but I thought I knew better. And you had no need to go to these elaborate lengths, you know—that very first time we met I would have walked over live coals for you.' Her mouth curled cynically. 'Rob was right, I was a stupid idealistic child, but not any longer—and before you say it, nothing you can say to me will convince me that my brother hurt your sister.' Her lips twisted. 'Women have been known to cry rape when all they've had is a change of heart, you know.'

For a moment she thought he was going to hit her, but he simply pushed past her and thrust open the door, turning just before it to say curtly, 'Get dressed and then we'll leave.'

CHAPTER THREE

SHE was in a dark labyrinth pursued by some terror that drew nearer with every breath, terrified because she could not find her way out. A door opened and a man stood there with his back to her. She felt a surge of joy and ran towards him. He turned and she started to scream and went on screaming because his face was the terror that stalked her.

The sound of her own screams woke Sienna from her nightmare. She was drenched in sweat, the bedclothes all tangled, her heart thumping uncomfortably. She glanced at her alarm. Two-thirty. She had been like this ever since that night at the cottage, suffering from this and other nightmares that prevented her from sleeping. She had lost weight too; Gill had noticed it and commented upon it, suggesting that she take some time off work, but that was the last thing she wanted to do. Work and sleep, they were the only ways she could escape from the torment of her thoughts. Two weeks had elapsed since it happened. Two weeks when only pride had kept her from pleading with Alexis, from throwing herself under the nearest bus and bringing a swift end to her pain.

The fact that Alexis had taken her virginity was something she could have come to terms with if he hadn't accomplished it by taking her heart; by allowing her to think herself loved, by deceiving her in the most cruel way it was possible for a man to deceive a woman. She writhed in a torment of self-mortification, of self-loathing for her folly in actually thinking he could care about her. Her naïvity, her trust, her sheer stupidity—these were the whips with which she flagellated herself mentally and from which there was no escape. She could hide her pain from the rest of the world, but she couldn't hide it from herself. She was fiercely glad that Rob was away, that at least when she returned to the flat in the evening she didn't have to pretend. Most nights she just sat staring into space, trying not to think or feel, while all the time her agony demanded an outlet. She was fiercely determined not to let herself grieve or mourn her own plight. She deserved it and had brought it upon herself with her own stupidity. If she hadn't been such a fool, believing herself in love and loved in return, none of it would ever have happened. It was her fault. She wasn't eating. The thought of food totally nauseated her, and she was glad that Alexis had left the country. She didn't even dare to walk past the Savoy in case she weakened and went in.

There were times when she wanted to scream out loud, to cry until there were no tears left. Times when she wanted to beg and plead, when she would have done anything for the comfort of his arms, the warmth of his body. And there were also times when she wanted to see him suffer as she was doing, when she felt tainted by the dark torment of her thoughts.

She grew thin and pale, quiet and reserved—and she also grew up. Other people grew to adulthood slowly, a gradual, relatively easy progress. She had remained a foolish trusting child, mentally at least, for far too long. Rob had been right when he said living with their father blinded her to real life, but all that was over now. Now she was a full fledged adult. Sometimes she felt as though she were two completely different people—the Sienna who smiled, worked, responded as others expected her to do in a rational calm manner, and the other Sienna, the one who was so emotionally crippled that she couldn't allow anyone to see or touch her, the one who cowered away from the slightest contact with other human beings, the one who cried out in the night a name which the other Sienna had forbidden her ever to utter.

But in one thing she remained steadfast. Nothing would convince her that Rob had so much as harmed a hair of Alexis' sister's head. She was so sure of her brother's innocence that she knew she wouldn't even ask him about it. There was a certain amount of savage satisfaction to be found in that thought. No doubt Alexis expected her to rush to Rob with the story of her humiliation at his hands, but she had made up her mind that no one, no one was going to know what had happened between them. If she could have arranged for her memory to wipe free that part of her life which involved him she would have done so and gladly.

Two and a half weeks after that final night with Alexis, Rob returned. He looked tanned but had lost weight, his hair bleached blond at the ends. He arrived just after she returned from work, wearing jeans and a thin shirt, shivering in the cool May breeze and complaining about the change of temperature. 'The eternal curse of roving reporters—colds and jet-lag,' he pronounced as he dropped down into a chair and studied her, his gaze sharpening as he took in the fragility of her pale face and the extreme slenderness of her body. 'You don't look too well yourself. What's the matter?'

'Nothing. I suppose I'm just coming to terms with Dad's death.' It was the excuse she offered everyone who commented on her loss of weight. 'Tell me about your trip.' She wanted to change the subject, and Rob seemed quite willing to oblige.

'I know we complain about this country, but some of these places. . . .' He shook his head wearily. He had been in El Salvador, and although he had assured her before he left that he would be in no danger she had worried about him. 'You don't look at all well,' he repeated, suddenly frowning as she stood up and he saw how baggy her jeans had become. 'Almost haunted. . . . What is it, Sienna? Or is it too private to talk about with a mere brother?'

'Oh, it's nothing,' Sienna assured him with forced airiness. 'I guess I'm just growing up.'

'At twenty-four—left it a bit late, haven't you? I've always thought of you as particularly mature.'

'Umm . . . well, you know what they way about growing pains, the older you are the more they hurt.'

'Do they? Well, I can tell when no trespassing signs are being posted, but just remember that I'm always here, and you can always talk to me, won't you?'

'Yes, big brother.' It took a considerable effort to make the flip retort and the grin that accompanied it, but it seemed to have the desired effect, because Rob's face lightened in obvious relief, and knowing that Alexis would think himself cheated of his revenge because Rob didn't know about it was a kind of balm to her tormented feelings.

Even so she was glad when Rob announced that he was going to have to go away again. 'You aren't eating enough,' he told Sienna, 'so tonight, I'm taking you out.'

'Oh, Rob, I really don't want to. . . .' she began, but he shook his head.

'No excuses, you're coming.'

'How long will you be gone this time?' she asked.

'I don't know. They're having some problems in Beirut and I'm being sent out to cover them. Look, Sienna, why don't you have a short holiday? Gill tells me you've been doing the work of two girls these last couple of weeks. Take a few days off. Go home and rest.'

She wanted to tell him that rest was the last thing she wanted; that work was the only thing she had to counteract her pain, but seeing his concern for her and not wanting to worry him any further, she forced a weak smile. 'Perhaps I will. There's still a lot of Father's papers and diaries I haven't touched. I could start going through those. Professor Grange wanted me to. He thinks there might be enough material there for another book and. . . .'

'I said you needed a rest, not more work,' Rob pointed out mildly. 'Leave the diaries, I'll try and read through them when I get back. I've got a month's leave due.'

'Well if one of us does need a holiday I suspect it's you,' Sienna told him. She wanted to suggest that he include Gill in their dinner date, but was reluctant to tread on what she suspected was very dangerous ground. Gill had made no secret of the fact that she would like Rob to give up his job. She worried constantly about the danger he was in and had told Sienna privately that she wanted a husband who shared her life, not a visitor whom she saw briefly for a handful of days out of every month, and while Sienna could not argue with her views, she also sympathised with Rob who she knew thrived on the danger of his job. If there was a problem only Rob and Gill could sort it out, and it wasn't up to her to meddle.

'Mmm, very nice.' Sienna was wearing the black dress with the matching jacket she had worn on her first dinner date with Alexis. She hadn't wanted to wear it, but there was nothing else suitable in her wardrobe, and what was the point of being stupidly sentimental? What was the point in deluding herself any more than she had already done so? There had been nothing romantic about her dates with Alexis, they had simply been a series of carefully calculated moves on the chessboard that was his life, a means to an end.

'You don't look bad yourself,' Sienna quipped back. And it was true. Rob looked extremely attractive in his formal dark suit and the pale silk shirt she had bought him for his birthday several weeks before.

She didn't talk as he drove through the wet city streets, too wrapped up in thoughts she knew it would have been wiser to dismiss. It had been raining all day and now a wet, grey dusk permeated the landscape, matching her dismal mood. It was only when they pulled up outside the Savoy that she recognised their destination, and a small moaned protest which Rob fortunately mistook for suprise left her parted lips.

'I thought tonight we'd push the boat out in style,' he told her cheerfully, handing her from the car and directing her towards the main entrance. 'It's years since I came here last. My godfather brought me once as a special treat.' Rob's godfather was a colleague of their father's who had gone into industry midway through his life and who had additionally received a life peerage for his work. When he left the university he and her father had lost touch, but Sienna dimly remembered him. 'What's the matter?' Rob demanded when they got inside and he saw Sienna's strained features for the first time. 'Aren't you feeling well?'

'I'm fine.' How could she spoil Rob's treat by asking to be taken home? She had to pull herself together, she told herself desperately. She couldn't go on for the rest of her life avoiding all the places she had been with Alexis. As always when she was tempted to remember how she had felt about him she made herself re-live those moments in the cottage when she had learned the truth, lashing herself mentally for her weakness, making herself remember that the love she had been stupid enough to believe existed had simply been a chimera: the result of her own foolish imagination.

The dining room was relatively full and in spite of her firm intentions Sienna found herself scouring the room for Alexis' familiar dark head. To her relief it wasn't there, but then why should it be? He had told her himself that he was going to New York, probably to make sure she didn't create any embarrassing scenes, she thought sardonically. No doubt he was adept at avoiding the women he had cast off when he no longer had any use for them, but she would never give him the satisfaction of letting him see again how completely he had destroyed her. She would never beg for the crumbs from his table, for the caresses she knew could only be given in pity and contempt.

They were shown to their table, the menus produced with a flourish. Sienna studied hers indifferently, trying to show an excitement she could not feel. Rob was plainly so delighted with his treat that she felt she had to try to respond to his mood. In the end she let him order for her, telling him that she wanted to be surprised. He raised his eyebrows a little but made no comment. His years as a journalist had given him a sophistication she hadn't previously witnessed. Her brother was a very attractive man, Sienna recognised absently, a man, she realised, who would be perfectly at home no matter what his surroundings.

Their first course arrived, and Rob, knowing of her preference for seafood, had ordered her a concoction of prawns and baked avocado, which she was surprised to discover was quite delicious. Nothing lasts for ever, she reminded herself, the human body can only pine for so long before nature reasserts herself, and after all those days of being unable to eat, suddenly she was hungry again.

Their wine arrived, the waiter poured it, and Sienna was just reaching out for her glass when she saw the group entering the dining room. In that second she knew she had deceived herself that she was beginning to get over Alexis. Merely looking at him brought a wave of mingled anguish and hatred so strong that she was surprised he didn't feel the waves of antipathy emanating from her. He was walking into the restaurant, another couple at his side, a young woman, who was laughing up at him, and another man, shorter, stockier than Alexis and completely without his charisma. Her heart thumping, unable to draw her eyes away from them, Sienna watched their approach. Alexis hadn't seen her, he was too busy talking to the woman at his side. His mouth was curved in a tender smile that wrenched at Sienna's heart, his whole attitude towards this other woman one of caring protection.

They were shown to a table not far from their own and as the girl took the proffered menu Sienna saw the huge sapphire glittering on her left hand. A rage of anger, so intense that she almost literally saw red, flooding through her body. She wondered if that girl knew what Alexis was really like. Who was she? The daughter of a fellow tycoon? She looked Greek—more so than Alexis himself.

'Sienna. . . .' With a start she realised that Rob had been talking to her and she hadn't heard a word. The timely arrival of the waiters with their main course gave her the opportunity to regain a little self-control, although she was acutely conscious of Alexis seated not three yards away, arrogantly oblivious to her presence. But then why should he be aware of it? As far as he was concerned her part in his life was finished. She had never been important to him as a person, in her own right, merely as Rob's sister. She glanced at her brother and was surprised to discover that he was staring at Alexis' table, his forehead pleated in a frown. For one hideous moment Sienna wondered if Alexis had been right and Rob had been involved with Alexis' sister, but almost instantly she dismissed the thought, startled by the sudden scraping sound of a chair, every muscle in her body tensing.

Rob was standing up, smiling, and then Sienna heard a husky accented feminine voice exclaiming with obvious pleasure, 'Rob, I thought it was you. How lovely to see you!' The woman who had been with Alexis was standing by their table embracing her brother, her dark eyes smiling. 'Constantin, Alexis, do come and be introduced to an old acquaintance. Rob, let me introduce you to my brother and my fiancé. Rob and I met in Sardinia, when we were staying at our villa there. He was doing an article on the local bandits.'

'Sofia, there is no need to pretend. I know that King was the one who . . . who hurt you.' That was Alexis' voice, and Sienna couldn't bring herself to look at him. Sofia, he had said, so that meant that the effervescent, laughing girl smiling at her brother was Alexis' sister and the fiancé she had mentioned must be the other man, who was now standing gravely to one side. At Alexis' words a tense silence enveloped them all. Sofia looked from her brother's set face to the sympathetic understanding one of her fiancé and then flushed a little as she glanced at Rob. 'Alexis, please.' Her voice was husky with pain, and out of the corner of her eye Sienna saw Constantin step forward, his arm supporting her. Sienna glanced up at her brother. Nearly as tall as Alexis, he was frowning, patently not understanding what was going on. Constantin murmured something to Sofia in Greek too low for Sienna to catch, then Sofia was touching her brother's arm, her voice unsteady as she whispered, 'Alexis, surely you did not believe that Rob was the one who . . . who attacked me? We were just friends. We. . . .'

'You met him every day, even though I had forbidden you to do so,' Alexis said curtly. 'You were betrothed to Nico at the time. . . .'

'A betrothal *I* did not want. Rob was a friend, someone to talk to who understood how trapped and despairing I felt.'

'He was also the man who. . . .' Sienna saw Alexis glare at her brother, a dark tide of colour surging up under his skin, as he muttered something in Greek. For a moment Sienna thought he meant to hit Rob, and it was obvious that Sofia and Constantin shared her fears, because they both moved forward, standing between Alexis and Rob. 'This is not the time to discuss such matters,' Alexis said curtly. His jaw was clenched and Sienna saw the small muscle that beat sporadically there as he looked across at her, probably wondering why she had said nothing to Rob of what he had done to her, Sienna thought bitterly. Had he really thought she could concede victory to him so easily?

'But I say it is,' Sofia said bravely. 'For too long the subject has been avoided between us. Constantin knows the whole of it.' She looked at her fiancé and such a look of love passed between them that Sienna felt a small lump rise in her throat. Constantin might not have Alexis' looks or personality, but it was plain that Sofia loved him and that her love was returned. 'I should have told you at the time, Alexis, but I was so shocked . . . you were so angry . . . I never dreamed you blamed Rob.' She glanced apologetically towards him. 'I am so sorry to involve you in this, my friend, especially when you are dining with such an attractive companion, but in view of my foolish brother's suspicions. . . .'

'Do you deny that you spent nearly every afternoon with him for an entire fortnight?' Alexis demanded. He looked so angry that Sienna wondered at Sofia's lack of concern. 'Do you really expect me to believe that in all that time ... that he was not the one who ...' he broke off, plainly fighting for self-control. 'Protect him as much as you choose, Sofia, but it is no use. Theo told me the truth. He saw the two of you together.'

'Theo!' For a moment Sofia's face was bleak, her pretty mouth twisted and bitter. 'Oh, yes, you would believe Theo, wouldn't you, Alexis? Your dear friend who meant so much to you. Did you never wonder why I didn't weep when his plane crashed? Well, I shall tell you why. It was because I had prayed that he would be punished, that he would suffer as he made me suffer. Theo was the man who attacked me and abused me, Alexis. I couldn't tell you at the time because he was your friend and you trusted him. But I never liked him. The only reason I agreed to the betrothal with Nico was because I was afraid that otherwise you might give me to Theo.'

Sienna found she had been holding her breath. She had never for one moment believed her brother guilty, and now, hearing him vindicated by the one person who had the knowledge to vindicate him brought no feeling of relief or pleasure. There was no wild surge of delight because Alexis had been proved wrong, just a vast empty nothingness, in which the voices of the others reached her, slightly distorted as though they had travelled a great distance. She was aware of Rob speaking, saying something to Alexis, and Alexis ignoring him to turn to Sofia and demand hoarsely, 'Is this the truth? You are telling me the truth?'

Truth, lies—what did it matter? Certainly it didn't matter to her, Sienna thought painfully. The room was starting to blur around her and then sway. She was conscious of a dark-suited arm reaching out towards her, and a concerned, kind pair of eyes watching her while their owner spoke; something soft and fluid in Greek that brought the attention of everyone else to her. Sofia was apologising to Rob for disrupting his meal, Rob was smiling away her apology. Any minute now and he would be introducing them, Sienna thought wildly, and that was something she couldn't endure. She couldn't bear to so much as look at Alexis. She tried to speak and found herself shivering convulsively.

'You must excuse us,' she heard Rob saying 'My sister isn't well. No, no . . . nothing for which you need feel guilty,' he was assuring Sofia. 'She hasn't been well for some time. The strain of my father's death, I suspect. Sienna . . . Sienna. . . .'

He was her one rock in the shifting dangerous sands on which she was standing and she clung selfishly to him, letting him help her to her feet, letting him talk over her head to Constantin and Sofia, letting him say the words that would get her out of the restaurant and away from Alexis.

'I'm sorry about all that.' They were back in the flat, and Rob had just walked through from the kitchen carrying a mug of Horlicks. 'Strange meeting Sofia like that after so long. It must be two years since we met in Sardinia.'

'Were you in love with her?'

Rob grimaced. 'Ordinary mortals don't dare to raise their eyes to members of the Stefanides clan, especially not the only sister of its leader! She was going through a difficult time. She'd been educated in Europe, and then had to go home and find herself having to contend with an arranged marriage. She needed someone to talk to, and I just happened to be there.'

'Did she ... did you know....'

'About her being attacked?' Rob shook his head. 'I'm presuming that for "attacked" I ought to substitute the word raped.' He grimaced again. 'Hardly flattering to discover that I'm supposed to have committed an atrocity like that, and our relationship was quite innocent, completely platonic. Anyone could see that she was an innocent, and knowing there was no future in it for us I deliberately didn't try for anything more than friendship. One thing puzzles me, though.' He was frowning, and Sienna felt her heart still for a moment before it started to thud heavily against her ribs. 'If Stefanides really thought I'd raped her, why didn't he come after me? No, I'm serious,' Rob assured her when he saw Sienna's face. 'You may not know it, but in Greece a girl's virginity is still very important. And to actually commit rape! Believe me, they have some pretty nasty ways of showing their disapproval. An accident, even a fatal one, would have been quite easy for a man of his wealth to organise.' He shrugged. 'Funny business altogether. I don't think I've ever seen a man look as shocked as he looked tonight when Sofia told him the truth.'

'I expect it was because he discovered that a man whom he obviously thought of as a friend and trusted had done it,' Sienna said colourlessly. She ought to be feeling pleasure in Rob's vindication, in Alexis' shock, but she couldn't. She couldn't feel anything other than a weak exhaustion. Now she was glad that Gill hadn't been with them to recognise Alexis and possibly alert Rob's suspicions. 'At least Sofia seems happy now,' Sienna murmured, draining her mug and putting it on one side. 'Constantin is obviously deeply in love with her.'

'Yes, he's a widower, and apparently an enlightened member of the species. I still can't get over the fact that Stefanides didn't come gunning for me when he thought I'd raped her. He's an extremely wealthy and powerful man. He could have done anything, ruined my career, caused me a fatal accident—anything. When I think about it it makes my blood run cold. In some parts of Greece they still practise vendetta. If he'd chosen to do so, none of us would have been safe, not Dad, not you. . . .' Rob's eyes darkened. 'Strangely enough, I think I can guess how he must have felt when he thought I had raped her. If any man hurt you, despite the fact that we're supposed to be civilised, I think I'd tear him apart!' He laughed, but Sienna was conscious of feeling deadly cold. Rob had been quite serious, and if he ever discovered just how badly she had been hurt and by whom . . . but Rob would never find out. He must never find out, because as he had just said, Alexis possessed the wealth and power to totally destroy him if Rob should ever try to strike out against him.

CHAPTER FOUR

'No!' Sienna awoke with a start, sitting bolt upright in the bed, her body rigid with rejection, every muscle tensed. With a slight sigh she exhaled, and glanced out of the window at the familiar view she had seen every morning on waking throughout her childhood and adolescence. It ought to have reassured and relaxed her, but it didn't. Her nightmares had become a nightly occurence since that fateful meeting at the Savoy, and always took the same form. Alexis would approach her on some pretext and ask her if she loved him. Her answer was always the same and she shivered in her thin nightdress, angry with herself for not being strong enough to withstand their potent aura of menace. It was nearly a week since that night. She ought to be over the shock of it by now. If she had needed any further convincing that Alexis simply wasn't interested in her surely she had received it. Not once during that meeting had he so much as glanced in her direction. Her mouth tightened in a rare grimace of cynicism. How did he feel now knowing that Rob had never touched his sister? Ashamed? Remorseful? Strange how the thought of seeing him humbled brought her so little pleasure, but then since that night at the cottage she had come to believe she had gone beyond feeling either pleasure or pain. They were emotions that belonged to the naïve girl she had been, not the woman she was now.

Her days had developed their own routine following her arrival at the village. She got up and dressed in old jeans and a Rugby shirt that had once belonged to Rob, made herself a cup of coffee, deciding against any breakfast. Her appetite was still very meagre, and she hadn't lost that haunted, grief-stricken look which had so worried her brother and Gill.

Carrying her mug of coffee, she made her way to her father's study, and sat down in the chair which had once been his. She was meticulously listing all his books—some of them were valuable first editions, and the time-consuming task of listing them kept her busy.

That it was a form of therapy she was quite well aware, and she even found the detachment to be slightly amused by her own obsessive care of her self-imposed task. Detachment was what she craved these days. Detachment offered safety, relief from the pain of loving too much and giving that love unwisely. Her old friends found her changed and had been quick to say so. She had been asked out several times by men she had known before she left for London, but she had no desire for their company. No desire for anyone's company, if the truth were known, she thought wryly, examining an exquisitely bound book, and checking it carefully before adding to her list. Her mental vulnerability reminded her sharply of how she had felt as a child after a bad bout of 'flu. She was experiencing in a mental context this time that same inability to rely on the reactions of her own body, that shaky insecurity that denoted the convalescent—but surely convalescing was a sign of recovery? She had been hurt, and badly, but no one would ever be able to hurt her like that again.

It was over—a closed chapter of her life, and now in this time of gathering her strength and assessing herself she must try to choose what she wanted to do with the rest of her life. She had never been particularly career-conscious, but perhaps that was what she needed, something to absorb every ounce of energy she had, something that demanded a total commitment.

She heard the front door open and sighed. Mrs Mallors, their neighbour, had been very good at keeping an eye on the house while it was empty, but she had also developed a rather trying habit of walking in unannounced, for a 'little chat', as she termed it. She was a widow and lonely, and Sienna knew she meant well, but she found it too difficult to relate to other people to want her company. She wanted to withdraw completely into herself and be left alone. All her energy was concentrated on healing her inner wounds; there was nothing left to spare for anyone else. But Mrs Mallors had been extremely good about looking after the house, and she couldn't totally ignore her, much as she wanted to.

Getting up, Sienna walked over to the door and opened it, forcing herself to smile, her smile rapidly fading as she found herself face to face, not with Mrs Mallors but with Alexis.

Her first instinct was to retreat behind the door and bolt and bar it against him, but he anticipated her urge to flee by walking past her inside it so that she had no option but to follow him, closing it after them.

'What are you doing here?'

Strange how mundane her first words to him should be! So trite and easily anticipated. She forced herself to look at him, fighting down the sickeningly acute feelings of pain surging through her.

His mouth twisted a little in something she took to be mockery, and she flushed despite her resolutions. He looked so tall and formidable in the small confines of her father's study, a remote stranger whose life had briefly touched her own, changing its course for ever.

'What do you think? I tried to contact you at the flat and the agency.' She had told Gill she was taking a few days' holiday, only Rob knew where she was, but of course Alexis had studied their family life and would have known where to find her. 'We have to talk.'

'Not as far as I'm concerned.' She turned her back on him, returning the volume she had been studying to the shelves, and reaching for another. Something in the quality of his silence disturbed her, a prescience that he wasn't simply going to go. 'I have nothing to say to you, Alexis,' she told him coldly. '*I* never believed Rob was guilty of raping your sister, you know that.'

'Yes.' His assent fell heavily into the thick silence. 'But until I heard her say it, I did not know that he was not Sofia's attacker.'

'No, you just assumed it was Rob,' Sienna agreed bleakly, wondering how she could appear so calm and civilised when inside she was still bleeding to death from the wounds he had inflicted. Pride and pride alone kept her from screaming her hatred at him, from wanting to wound and maim him as he had done her. 'Sofia was too shocked at the time of the . . . attack to answer my questions. I knew that she was seeing your brother, he was older than her, far more experienced, from a different race, it seemed natural to suppose. . . .'

'And on the strength of that supposition you planned the method of your revenge,' Sienna said quietly. 'There really was no need to come all the way down here to tell me that, Alexis. Contrary to the impression of my intelligence I must have given you by being so gullibly easy to seduce, I *am* quite able to draw the correct conclusions from what Sofia said. I never believed for one moment that Rob had hurt your sister,' her head lifted proudly, brown eyes squarely meeting grey across the width of the room, 'and not merely because he is my brother.'

'You haven't told him what happened?'

'No. There was no point.' She bit her lip, remembering what Rob had said about wanting to tear any man who harmed her apart. 'It might interest you to know, though, that he shares your views—at least on the subject of sisters. He was surprised that you hadn't tried to hurt him in some way—through his job perhaps. He said you were rich enough to have accomplished it. I didn't disillusion him.'

'Why not?'

'Because I don't want him to get hurt.' She said the words softly, and watched him pale a little beneath his tan. 'And besides, no matter what he did, it can't put things right, can it? Sofia is lucky to have found a man like Constantin who obviously loves and cherishes her.'

'Is that what you want? The safe harbour of marriage to a man who cares enough for you not to mind that he is not your first lover?'

'I don't want to be any man's lover,' Sienna replied flatly, her eyes betraying all that she didn't want him to see, and his own leapt and hardened in recognition of what she was feeling, smouldering with an intensity that stopped the breath in her lungs and infused the room with a subtle sense of menace.

'You're lying,' Alexis said smokily. 'You wanted my love, Sienna. You begged me for it,' he reminded her cruelly.

She wanted to scream out with the pain he was causing her, but the new Sienna, the one who had taken the place of that girl, simply said calmly, 'Yes, I know, but you see that was before I realised how naïve I was. I don't believe you're capable of loving anyone, Alexis. Your insufferable sense of pride wouldn't allow you to. Oh, I don't doubt you have desired and will desire very many women, and that you make love to them expertly, even perhaps deceive them into thinking you genuinely care, but I don't believe you do. No man who really cares about women could do to one what you did to me.'

'You came to me willingly.' His face was tight with anger. It glittered in his eyes and was betrayed in the grim compression of his jaw, but strangely enough she wasn't afraid any longer. 'Yes,' she agreed quietly, 'and that's what I mean. I can't argue with your claim that you had to use me because of the crime you believed my brother committed, but you weren't satisfied with that, were you Alexis? You wanted to add a little refinement, to torture and then humiliate me by allowing me to fall in love with you. . . .'

Her mouth curled contemptuously. 'No man who really likes and admires women would have done a thing like that, and to me it betrays what you think of my whole sex. Even your own sister couldn't confide in you, not even the name of the man who attacked her, because he was your friend and she feared that you would believe him before you believed her.'

She knew that her words had found their mark. His skin looked grey beneath its healthy tan, and his eyes were bleak, darkening with a pain she could only guess at, but she refused to feel pity for him.

'I came here today to apologise to you, to try and. . . .'

'And what?' she taunted. 'Wipe out what happened? Don't you think if that was possible I would have already done it? No matter how much you regret it, Alexis, you can't regret it one quarter as much as I do. Now please leave.' She walked over to the door and held it open, tensing when he refused to move.

'I haven't said all I came here to say yet,' he began tersely, but Sienna refused to listen. Suddenly the adrenalin which had kept her going since his arrival deserted her, leaving her sick and shaking.

'Very well,' she said bitterly, 'if you won't leave, then I will.' She turned for the door before he could stop her, throwing it open and fled through the hall, panicked by the sound of his footsteps behind her, hard and determined. The house only had a short front garden which bordered on the narrow main road, curling through the village. Sienna felt the latch on the gate give under her fingers, and her eyes darkened with fear as she glanced over her shoulder and saw Alexis striding towards her, determination in every line of his face. Thrusting open the gate, she stepped out into the road, the sound of Alexis' voice calling her name mingling with the squeal of car brakes and tyres. She had a brief impression of a glittering bonnet and beyond it a man's face, contorted with horror, and then the world exploded in pain, wave after wave of it, flooding over her carrying her to a place where nothing else could possibly reach her.

She opened her eyes slowly, aware of confused impressions of a vague memory for some reason of the words of the Church of England marriage service, of a man's voice, deep and sure, saying, 'I do', and another, lighter, hesitant, her own, echoing the words, although every instinct she possessed screamed out that such a service could only be a dream. She was in a room, unlike any room she remembered, and which somehow she knew to be in a hospital, although she had no knowledge of how she came to be there. From her bed she could see through the window, skyscraper blocks and an intensely blue sky. The window was open and she could feel the heat wafting inwards, and something told her that she wasn't used to such high temperatures. Her door opened and a nurse came in, startled to find her awake. She disappeared before Sienna could speak, then returned with a man. Middle-aged and slightly stooped, he had an olive complexion and dark, intense eyes. He smiled at her, and said in English, 'So, you have decided to wake up properly at last.' He kept talking to her while he examined her, then stood back, smiling down at her. 'So. . . . Are you ready for a visitor?'

The door opened and another man walked in. Her eyes leapt to his dark, impassive and totally unfamiliar face, her heart twisting with a curious current of pain which seemed to run from the top of her body to the bottom. Fear tinged the pain and she stiffened without being aware of it, rejecting him with her eyes as he walked towards the bed. He stretched out and lifted her left hand. On it a diamond ring glittered, beside it a plain gold band. So she *was* married. Why should she feel she wasn't?

'Where am I?' she demanded huskily, struggling to sit up, overwhelmed by a sensation of panic. 'Who are you. . . .?'

He looked back at her without smiling. 'I'm your husband, Sienna.'

She could see the doctor frowning, and a feeling of deep despair, of being trapped and helpless, flooded through her. 'But I don't know you,' she protested. 'I don't know you!'

'Now, Mrs Stefanides, it's all right. You had an accident, and as a result. . . .'

'Thank you, Dr Theonstanis, but I will explain. If you would leave us for a moment.' The doctor frowned again, but signalled to his nurse to leave, following her to the door, and Sienna knew instinctively that he did not usually allow the relatives of his patients to dictate to him.

Stefanides, Theonstanis—these were Greek names, strange that she should know that, when she couldn't even remember her own, wouldn't have known it if this stranger who claimed to be her husband had not told her. She glanced down again at her left hand. The rings were new. How long had they been married? How long had she been lying here?

'Now. You have had an accident, and as a result you're suffering from amnesia. Nothing to worry about, it's quite a common occurrence.'

'But surely only when people want to forget something to begin with?' How had she known that? She stared up into the cold grey eyes searching her face, and shivered. How could she be married to this cold, frighteningly austere man? Marriage to her meant love, and she was sure love could never have existed between this stranger and herself. Her husband, the closest relationship two human beings could have, and yet he was a stranger to her.

'You're speaking to me in English,' she said huskily, 'but your name is Greek.'

'I am Greek,' he told her, 'but you are English.'

'How long . . . how long have we been married?' She returned to the subject of their marriage like someone probing an aching tooth, unable to accept its reality, overwhelmed by a feeling of frustration that she was totally reliant on this man to tell her the most basic things about herself.

'Not very long.'

'And my accident?' Her mouth was dry. Somehow she knew that her marriage and her accident were connected.

'Shortly after we were married.'

'Then. . . .'

'We have been lovers,' he supplied, watching her face, smiling grimly at the tide of colour that swept it.

'I . . . we. . . .' Suddenly she started to shake, her face as white as the cotton sheets on her narrow bed, her body tensing against his words. This man, this stranger, privy to the most intimate secrets of her body—it was more than she could bear!

'Sienna . . . Sienna, don't faint, damn you,' she heard him saying, but the words came from far away, too distant to reach into the warm secret place she had escaped to.

'So, you are with us again, young lady.' Her eyes

searched the room feverishly, but she was alone in it with the doctor. He seemed to guess at the reason for her tension and frowned, consulting a chart he was holding, then smiled at her when he perceived her anxiety.

'Am I ... am I going to be all right? My husband said I had an accident.'

'Yes, you will be fine,' he assured her. 'You are blessed with a particularly hard skull. Can you remember anything about your accident?'

Sienna shook her head. 'I can't remember anything, full stop. Where did it happen?'

'In England, so your husband told me. He brought you here to Greece, as soon as the doctors permitted him to have you moved. Tell me, can you remember anything at all? No, don't force yourself to remember ... it will all come back in time.'

'But why have I forgotten?' Her forehead pleated in a frown. 'Surely people suffering from amnesia forget because they want to forget, because there's something in their past they don't want to remember.'

'Not always. Could there be something in *your* past, do you think?'

'I don't know.' The effort of trying to remember exhausted and frustrated her. How could she tell this kind man that she was frightened because she didn't remember her husband, because something about him unnerved her and threatened to unleash emotions she wasn't sure she wanted to experience? 'We have been lovers,' he had said, and she had felt the effect of his words right through her body, as intimately as though he had reached out and touched her.

'Don't worry, it will all come back in time. Some

things quite automatically, like the way you speak English but can understand Greek when it is spoken slowly.'

'And the way I knew your name was Greek,' Sienna mused. 'Why is that?'

He shrugged. 'We are not sure. The mind is a complex and delicately balanced piece of equipment. Like a computer, to get the correct information out we have to punch the right information in. Amnesia is rather like speaking to a computer in the wrong language, but we will find the right one.'

'And if I don't want to remember?'

He frowned and tapped his pencil on the chart. 'Sometimes the mind uses amnesia as a form of protection, a scab over a sore, but eventually wounds heal, there will come a day when you no longer need the protection of forgetfulness, when you are strong enough to confront whatever it is you wanted to hide from.' He walked towards the door.

'Dr Theonstanis.' He paused and studied her unknowingly wan face. Alexis had asked to be told the moment she woke up from the shot they had given her after her faint, and he half expected to hear her ask for him, but instead she asked hesitantly, pleating the sheet with nervous fingers, 'Have I ... has anyone ... have I any other family, besides my husband, I mean?'

'I'm afraid I don't really know. Your husband gave me the English hospital notes on you when I took over your case. Physically you are fully recovered, and there is no reason why you shouldn't be discharged with the next few days. For the rest, I'm afraid you will have to ask him.'

'Discharged!' Fear raced through her. She didn't

want to be discharged into the power of this man who said he was her husband, whose rings she wore and who she was quite sure she didn't love. 'But surely my amnesia. . . .'

'That we will continue to treat, of course, but rest and relaxation are the main prescriptions. Your husband has a beautiful villa on the equally beautiful island of Micros, where he has assured me that you will have every care. My colleague there will visit you to check on your progress. I'm afraid in a case like yours we cannot chart how much progress you should make. Your memory might return slowly, or alternatively one day. . . .' he shrugged as though to signify his inability to qualify the possible term of her convalescence. 'And now I suppose you would like to see your husband. He has been like a tiger in a cage,' he told her with a slight grimace. 'All my nurses are in awe of him. I suspect he would have nursed you himself had we permitted it,' he added with a chuckle. 'Seldom have I seen so devoted a husband—but then you have not been married long and your accident, I understand, took place shortly after you were married.'

The picture he was painting did not accord with Sienna's brief memories of the man who claimed he was her husband. Devotion was not an emotion she would have thought familiar to him. He was too hard, too arrogant for such a timid, selfless description. The doctor had reached the door, and she wanted to plead with him not to permit Alexis to see her, but it was already too late. The door was open and he was walking towards her. Her eyes registered the close-fitting cream jeans and the thin silk shirt that went with it. Through it she could see the tracery of dark hairs shadowing his chest and her body reacted with a wave of nausea she could barely control, her body shaking, drenched in perspiration.

'Sienna!' Instantly he was at her side, pushing her down on the bed, touching her moist skin, and frowning in the direction of the doctor as though he were the culprit. 'What is the matter with her?' he demanded peremptorily. 'She is shivering, and the temperature in here is well into the seventies!'

'A sudden spasm of weakness. Your wife has been very ill. It is natural that she should be afraid.'

'Afraid?' Grey eyes raked her pale face, the thin mouth tightening imperceptibly. 'Are you trying to tell me she is frightened of me? Her husband?'

'You are a stranger to her,' the doctor reminded him gently. 'It is only natural that she should feel fear.'

'Is that true?' Alexis demanded when they were alone. 'You are frightened of me?'

'I don't know you.' Sienna moved away from his constraining hand.

'Ah, but you do, Sienna.' His voice was soft, rich with sensual meaning and she flushed vividly as hot as she had been cold. 'We know each other in the most intimate sense of the word. You are my wife.'

'But we haven't been married very long.'

'And because of that you think I have not taken you to my bed?' He laughed softly. 'What makes you think I waited for the wedding ceremony?' He was holding her hand and he lifted it to his mouth kissing her trembling fingers, his eyes defying her to look away from him. 'Your mind may not remember me, Sienna, but your body recognises me.' He bent his head and pressed his lips to the pulse thudding at the base of her throat, and immediately, scorchingly, Sienna knew that he hadn't lied. Impossible though it was for her to comprehend, her body did recognise him, and yielded to him on a weak tide of pleasure that surged along her veins.

'Soon I shall be taking you home, and there I will show you just how much pleasure our bodies take in each other.' He stood up, releasing her hand, but Sienna barely noticed, frowning deeply as something he had said rang a warning bell in her mind. If only she could remember . . . if only she wasn't lost in this fog of unknowingness, totally reliant on this man all her senses warned her not to trust, for every signpost back to the past.

'I asked the doctor if I had any family . . . besides you,' she managed painfully, 'but he didn't know.'

'You have a brother.' He watched her carefully, but Sienna felt no spark of response. 'He is working abroad at the moment and I haven't been able to contact him to tell him about your accident.'

'You said we were married?'

'In England, after what I believe is termed a whirlwind courtship.' He saw her look of disbelief and laughed, a half growl of sound deep in his throat. 'You do not believe me? I assure you it is true. I knew the moment I saw you that I had met my destiny. . . .'

'And me.'

'You?' He smiled deeply, indenting his mouth, laughter gleaming in his eyes. 'Ah, my Sienna, you fell in love with me on sight.' His fingers cupped her jaw, preventing her from looking away from him. 'You want to deny it, I can see it in your eyes, but it is true, I assure you. When I have you home and safe I will show you how true.'

'But I don't remember you. I. . . .'

Before she could say any more a nurse walked into the room looking briskly at her watch and then at Alexis.

'We can talk again later,' Alexis told her calmly. 'Rest now, and get better so that I can take you to Micros and you can recover in the warmth of our Greek sun.'

'Can the sun give me back my memory?' Sienna asked in angry frustration, but he refused to be drawn by or respond to her anger, and she was left alone with her nurse and her tempestuous, disturbing thoughts, and the clamouring of her senses which warned her that he was speaking the truth when he said they had been lovers. If they had been lovers she must care about him. She knew instinctively that she wasn't the kind of woman who would take pleasure in a chain of brief sexual encounters. No, when she gave her body it would only be with love, and she had given her body to him, she knew it with some instinct that went deeper than mere memory.

So why was she so antagonistic towards him, so defensive in his presence? Surely as her lover and her husband he would be the one person she would want to be with—and yet alarm bells rang consistently in her head whenever he came near her.

It was all too taxing to dwell on too much, her body and mind exhausted by the shock of discovering her lost memory defeated her efforts to concentrate, and she was grateful for the soothing drug the nurse offered her, bringing a sweet, dark oblivion, which was what she seemed to crave.

CHAPTER FIVE

'So, you are now ready to leave us.' Doctor Theonstanis seemed to think she ought to be pleased, but weak apathy would be a better description of her true feelings, weak apathy tinged with alarm, Sienna thought tiredly. It was true that over the last few days she had lost her dread of Alexis' visits. He was her husband and he was unfailingly kind to her. It wasn't, after all, his fault that she couldn't remember a single thing about him. Indeed he had shown remarkable patience, apart from one or two spine-tightening remarks about their lovemaking, and she owed it to him to greet the news that she could now go to Micros with him with something approaching enthusiasm. Having to stay close to the hospital in Athens with her must have severely disrupted his life. He must surely work, although she hadn't yet discovered what at, and there was a limit to the understanding of even the most patient of employers. And yet despite Alexis' patient manner toward her Sienna was aware of not feeling completely at ease in his company. Why should she feel like that? He was her husband, and one look at him had been sufficient to assure her that he was first and foremost very much a male man, who had presumably married her because he loved and desired her. They had been lovers, so he had told her, but she felt no sense of familiarity towards him. She wanted to plead with the doctor to allow her to remain in the hospital a little while longer, but common sense told her that that would simply be putting off the evil day. She couldn't play the invalid for the rest of her life.

As though he guessed her fears Dr Theonstanis had tried to reassure her, telling her that it was only natural that she should feel uncertain and nervous of leaving hospital, going out into a world which was essentially unfamiliar. 'Your husband tells me that you have never visited Micros,' he told her as he studied her.

'So there will be nothing there that will help me remember?'

'The memory is a strange thing,' he responded obliquely. 'We will see.'

She was dressed in the clothes Alexis had brought the previous day, sitting on the end of her bed, waiting for him when he arrived, her fingers stroking the soft silk of her cream dress. The dress and the silk underwear that went with it were luxuries for her, she knew that instinctively, and wondered if Alexis had spent lavishly on her in an effort to boost her spirits. As always when she saw him she was struck by the total maleness of his face and body, the same alien tremor she always experienced running through her body, colour mounting in her pale face as he watched her.

'Good,' he commented when his scrutiny was over. 'I see the dress fits. I wasn't too sure.'

'You ... you haven't bought clothes for me before?'

'In London there wasn't time, and then you have lost weight.'

'They're very expensive.' She touched the silk again. 'You shouldn't have spent so much. My own clothes. . . .'

He shrugged aside her protests indifferently,

saying only, 'It is much hotter here in Greece than you are used to. You had nothing really suitable for our climate, but if what I have chosen for you is not to your taste you can buy more the next time we come to Athens for your check-up. I've arranged for us to be flown to Micros. Normally I use my yacht, but the sea journey takes eighteen hours, and as this is the first time you have left your bed for any length of time. . . .'

'Will you be coming with me?'

He stared at her, and Sienna recognised with a sudden thump of her heart that despite all her fears and doubts about him, once she left the hospital he would be the only thing that was familiar in an otherwise alien world.

'Don't you want me to? Would you prefer to go alone, to a strange island, a strange house?'

Sienna shuddered as his words echoed her own thoughts, shaking her head. 'No, but I thought perhaps your work . . . your employers. . . .'

He smiled sardonically as though for some reason she had amused him, but said only, 'There is nothing you need to worry about. My place for the moment is with you.' His face hardened, cold and reserved, his thoughts hidden from her, but Sienna thought she heard him mutter, 'After all, it is my fault that you are here,' but before she could question him he was striding towards the small cupboard by her bed and removing her personal belongings, putting them in the case which had contained her new clothes. He grimaced faintly over the thick cotton nightdresses she had folded only that morning, and said wryly, 'I suppose we must take these with us. I suggest you give them to Maria—you certainly won't be needing them. I have not enjoyed seeing you lying in that narrow little bed dressed like a nun, only able to remember what it feels like to have you in bed beside me, your body curved against mine.'

As always when he mentioned anything intimate Sienna was aware of a confused mingling of embarrassment and apprehension, and she licked her lips nervously, studying him beneath her lashes, her voice faintly strained as she asked, 'Your house ... will we be alone there, or do you share it with other members of your family?' She knew that Dr Theonstanis shared his home with his mother and sisters and had learned that this was common practice in Greece, but Alexis shook his head decisively and said, 'My only family is my sister, who lives in New York. Maria and Georges look after the house for me, so you need not worry that I shall put you to work scrubbing and cooking the moment we arrive.'

'Between us then we seem remarkably short of relatives,' she managed dryly as he watched her. 'You have one sister and I have one brother. Have you been able to contact him at all?'

Alexis shook his head. 'Not yet, but as to our lack of family, *pethi mou*, that is something we can perhaps remedy ourselves.'

She saw the look in his eyes and her heart raced. 'You mean children?'

'You don't want to carry my child.' He crossed the room and came to stand in front of her, his grey eyes almost black as he watched the emotions chase one another across her pale face.

'No, it isn't that. . . .' How could she explain that although she knew instinctively that she liked and wanted children, she still found him too much of a stranger to contemplate with any degree of equanimity the degree of intimacy he was discussing?

'So, and it certainly can't be the getting of them that brings that look of terror to your eyes, for, as I have good cause to know, you are delightfully responsive in bed.'

Was she? She licked her lips again, flushing when she saw the way his eyes followed the brief gesture, their expression as old as time itself, the hard pad of his thumb reaching out to probe the slightly moist skin. She jerked away, trembling under his touch aware of the conflict of her emotions. She couldn't simply resume the married life they presumably had enjoyed before her accident, it would be like going to bed with a complete stranger, but when she tried, haltingly, to explain her feelings to him he simply laughed and said softly, 'So much the better, just think of all the things I shall have to teach you which I already know you enjoy.'

When she would have protested, he said sardonically, 'I am not going to permit you to sleep in a separate room from me, Sienna. I appreciate how difficult things are for you, but we have been lovers, we are married, I am not a patient man or a boy content to settle for courtship all over again. Listen to your body,' he told her softly, 'and not your mind. It will tell you how intimately we are known to one another.'

Her husky, 'No, I can't,' was stifled beneath the hard possession of his mouth, searing against her lips, silencing her protests. She tried to reject him, but he was too strong for her, arms like steel clamping her to him, strong fingers holding her face, the rhythmic stroke of his tongue against the swollen outline of her lips coaxing them to part in direct contradiction to her intentions. That they had kissed like this before she couldn't deny. She could feel it in the powerful surge of emotion that swept through her body, her fingers sliding into the thick darkness of his hair as he arched her back over his arm. Her skin burned where his mouth touched it and she shook violently in his arms as he trailed kisses along the curve of her throat and the deep V of her silk dress. His hand found her breast, probing the rounded contours, and Sienna wondered if he could feel the swift gallop of her heart as intensely as she could herself. She gasped in protest as his fingers found the buttons of her dress and the soft creamy swell of her breasts were exposed to his gaze. His thumb stroked over the fine silk of her bra, the fabric doing nothing to conceal the flaunting evidence of his effect on her, and Sienna heard him growl softly in his throat as she started to protest, a husky, masculine sound of satisfaction and pleasure as he pushed aside the silk barrier completely and she felt the burning scorch of his mouth against her skin. Deep shudders racked through her, an amalgamation of pleasure and shock, her eyes wide and unseeing as she stared up into his face, too stunned to do anything other than simply stand there as he pushed her gently away and then fastened the buttons of her dress. She tried to breathe and found it caused her physical pain. Her body shook with reaction and she turned away from Alexis, not wanting him to see how shocked she had been by the explosiveness of the feelings he had aroused inside her.

'You're an extremely sensual woman,' he told her calmly as though he had read her mind, 'and it's been a long time. . . .'

Muzzy and still half dazed with reaction, Sienna stammered, 'I didn't know, I never guessed. I. . . .' She sat down on the edge of her bed, gnawing on her bottom lip. Underlying the intense feeling of pleasure she had experienced at his touch had been a jagged-edged warning, an inner voice that urged her not to respond, and she couldn't understand why. They were married, they loved one another, and there should only have been cause for concern if she had not responded to him, not because she had.

'Something still worries you?' She looked up at him. He was her husband, the only key to the past she had. She took a deep breath. It was time she started behaving like an adult and not a frightened child.

'When you touched me, I felt as though it was wrong for me to respond. . . .' She shook her head, trying to grasp the elusive strands of memory which always remained just out of reach. 'I can't explain it properly, but it's as though I have to be on my guard with you.'

For a moment he simply stood staring out of the window, and Sienna wondered what thoughts were running through his mind. 'Dr Theonstanis says I mustn't jog your memory about the past. It has to come back naturally. But we are married, Sienna, and there is no reason in the world for you to fear that our marriage in any way is insecure. Trust me,' he asked quietly, 'that's all I shall ask.' He came across to her and tilted her chin so that she was forced to look up into his eyes. 'Will you do that? Will you give me your trust?'

She wanted to, so much, and when she nodded her assent it was as though she had laid down a heavy burden. Alexis slid his fingers into the thick hair at her nape, pushing her head down on to his shoulder, stroking and soothing her with hands that she knew instinctively would know how to give a woman pleasure.

'How did I have my accident?' She had wanted to ask the question before but somehow never dared.

'It was my fault.' She could sense the tension inside him. 'We had a quarrel and you ran out into the street. You were hit by an oncoming car. I thought I had lost you.'

'It's funny, the only thing I can remember is our wedding.' She felt his muscles tense and wondered if it was because she had said their wedding and not his lovemaking. 'The first thing I remembered when I came round properly was a hazy recollection of the marriage ceremony. Were we married in England?'

'Yes.' His voice was almost terse. 'Don't try to force yourself to remember, Sienna. It will happen in due course.' He glanced at his watch, and Sienna noticed that it was an expensive one. Hard on the heels of the thought she frowned. How had she known that? Dr Theonstanis had explained to her that the memory was a complex thing, that some things she would know and remember automatically, while others would elude her.

'Ready?'

She nodded, trying to quell the rising storm of butterflies taking wing in the pit of her stomach. Alexis had a car waiting, a black Mercedes which smelled of expensive leather. He must have a very good job, she thought, as he fastened the seat-belt for her, but when she voiced her thoughts his smile did not quite reach his eyes. Had they quarrelled in the past about money? She didn't think she was a particularly extravagant female, or one who placed a great deal of importance on wealth. It was what a man was that mattered, not what he had.

Athens was completely unfamiliar, the heat and the blare of sounds outside the car making her shrink unwittingly into the safety of her seat. Above them on the hill, she caught tantalising glimpses of the Acropolis, but Alexis shook his head when he saw her wistful expression. 'Another time,' he told her. 'You're well on the way to recovery but not yet strong enough for sightseeing in the full heat of our summer sun.'

'Summer?' He caught the surprise in her voice and said, 'Yes, you had your accident in May, it's now nearly the end of June. You were in a coma for several days initially and Dr Theonstanis tells me that the rest of the time you spent in hospital will probably never be more than a blur.'

'I was lucky I didn't break anything, I suppose.'

'Yes, if you count a fractured skull as "not breaking anything",' Alexis agreed sardonically, but there was pain as well as irony in his eyes when he looked at her, and that more than anything that had gone before buoyed her spirits. They were travelling by helicopter to Micros, and when she looked surprised Alexis said perfunctorily, 'The island is very small, my father bought it just after the war, and I was tempted to sell it when he and my stepmother were drowned just off the coast in their yacht, but Sofia didn't want me to, and I must admit that I'm glad I didn't too.'

'You own the island?' She breathed the words with awed disbelief, everything suddenly meshing into place, the fact that he could take unlimited time off work, the expensive watch and clothes he always wore, the dress and underwear he had bought for her. 'You're rich!'

'Don't say it as though you've suddenly discovered I've got typhoid,' Alexis said dryly. 'You look quite shocked.' He flicked a glance at her pale face and huge eyes. 'Not many women would look so disturbed to discover they were married to a wealthy man. Isn't that supposed to be every beautiful girl's goal?'

'Not mine,' Sienna said positively, knowing intuitively that it was true. 'I didn't marry you for your money.'

'No.' He said it dryly, and Sienna wondered what lay behind the brief agreement. Had there perhaps been a time when he had thought she had married him for his wealth? She knew with a knowledge that was deep-rooted that she herself had not come from a moneyed background, although she couldn't have pinpointed how she knew, but Alexis was an extremely shrewd and intelligent man and it was impossible to believe that he could ever assume any woman with eyes in her head would marry him purely for monetary reasons.

'Was that what we quarrelled about,' she asked awkwardly, 'money?'

'Quarrelled?' His voice was sharp and she shrank back under the sting of it. As though he realised that his tone upset her, he said in a softer voice. 'No, it wasn't about money. Although a man in my position does tend to become, shall we say, slightly sensitive about other people's motives. That's why I always like to come back to Micros. The people who live there live what I suppose could be termed a simple life, but it is one they are content with. The men are proud and the women content. Here we are.' He parked the car in silence, and helped her out of it, carrying her case as though it weighed no more than the soft leather clutch bag he had given her. The bag matched the soft cream shoes she was wearing, both unfamiliar to her, and there had been nothing inside her bag she could identify with. It had contained a lipstick, obviously brand new, a small palette of eyeshadow in what she suspected must be high fashion colours, some drachmas, a handkerchief and very little else.

When he realised that she was falling behind, Alexis matched his long stride to accommodate her shorter one, his hand under her elbow as he directed her towards the waiting helicopter. The pilot greeted him respectfully, and they exchanged a few sentences in Greek, although they spoke too quickly for her to understand more than a few words. Alexis helped her into the ungainly craft and got in beside her, smiling when she voiced her sudden fear that she would not be able to make herself understood to Maria and Georges.

'Don't worry, they both speak English, although you can understand Greek.'

'Did you teach me?' It was an automatic and quite natural question and she wasn't prepared for the way he frowned, his eyes suddenly dark and his mouth forbidding.

'You can ask me that question again tonight when I hold you in my arms and listen to your love words.'

They had met in London, Alexis had told her, and when they were airborne Sienna found herself wondering how they had met. He was a very wealthy man and she, she was sure, was a relatively ordinary mortal, so how had their paths crossed—and not merely crossed, but continued together? London. . . . She closed her eyes and tried to think, but as always when she tried to recapture the past there was nothing, nothing but an aching sense of frustration and a renewal of the horror she had felt when she first discovered she had lost her memory.

It would all come back to her in time, Dr Theonstanis had told her, but what if it didn't; what if she was condemned to a lifetime of not knowing anything more about herself than she knew now? Her parents, her family, her growing up—what had they been? She must have made a small sound of despair, because Alexis turned towards her and touched her cheek. Her eyes flew open and met his.

'I was trying to remember,' she told him wretchedly, 'but I can't, I *can't*!'

'You will. Look down below and you will see the first of the islands. . . .' She allowed him to change the subject. Obviously her loss of memory must be as worrying to him as it was to her. She had hardly behaved towards him as a loving wife. That was something she must try to correct, she told herself firmly. Alexis was right, she must listen to her body, not her mind. He struck her as an intensely physical and virile man, one who would expect the woman in his life to share his pleasure in lovemaking. Which presumably she had done, so why did she feel this frisson of—well, apprehension tinged with something that bordered on anger against herself at the thought that she might? The apprehension was understandable perhaps—after all, Alexis was now a stranger to her, but the other. . . . Sienna gnawed at her bottom lip. Why should she feel that in making love with Alexis she was going against some inner rule that urged her at all costs to hold him at bay?

'There's Micros down below, to the left. Look, can you see it?' She had to move closer to Alexis to gaze in the direction he was indicating, the hard warmth of his thigh pressed against hers, the contact brief, but disturbing. So much so that she was glad to be able to draw away when she had finally picked out the small island.

When they drew nearer and she saw how small and remote Micros actually was she glanced nervously at Alexis. 'Something wrong?'

'No. I was just thinking how tiny Micros looks—how remote. Wouldn't it have been better if we had stayed in Athens, at least until. . . .' She floundered badly when she saw the expression in his eyes. He knew quite well why she was having second thoughts, and they had nothing to do with the inaccessibility of the island and everything to do with the knowledge that she would virtually be alone on it with him.

'We would have been equally alone in my penthouse suite,' he told her suavely, confirming that she had read his glance correctly, 'but Athens is hot and crowded at this time of year. Doctor Theonstanis and I both thought the island would be better for you. It has the benefit of a cooling breeze and its beaches are quite safe. The Aegean is very pleasant to swim in.'

Swim? Yes, she would enjoy that! Sienna frowned as the thought winged its way through her mind. How was it she could remember that she could swim, but until he walked into her hospital room that morning she hadn't been able to remember the slightest thing about her husband?

'Alexis, were we happy together?' she asked him impulsively, ignoring his swift frown as he looked back at her. 'Please . . .' she begged. 'I can't help worrying about the fact that I can't remember you. You're my husband, we've been lovers, but. . . .'

She saw that she had angered him and blamed her tactlessness. In his shoes would she have welcomed hearing that he could not remember her? 'Dr Theonstanis has already told you, you will remember when you are ready.' As she subsided into her seat once more Sienna realised that he had not answered her question, but she knew she would not repeat it. 'Tell me about your sister,' she said instead, 'about your childhood.'

For a moment she thought he meant to refuse, then he shrugged carelessly. 'Sofia is living in New York with her husband now. She is ten years younger than me. My father was married twice, but neither marriage was what you would term in Europe "happy". He married my mother because she brought with her a good dowry, and he married Sofia's because he wanted more than one son. My mother died in childbirth, and as I have said, Sofia's was drowned off the coast of Micros with my father.'

'You must have missed him dreadfully,' Sienna said sympathetically, but he shrugged her concern aside, his attention on the island taking shape below them.

'Not really. He and I were never very close. After I left university he wanted me to join him in his business—I had other ambitions, but I was his only son, in Greece that is a very close bond, and when he was killed I had no choice. Sofia was barely twelve and my responsibility.'

'What would you have done, if you hadn't had to take over the business?' Sienna enquired, curiously.

'Who knows? I wanted to buy a schooner and

sail it round to the West Indies, perhaps do some charter work, anything other than sit in an office directing the business my father had built up.'

If he was ten years older than Sofia he must have been twenty-two when his father was drowned, a young age to take on the responsibility of a teenage sister and a business empire. Was it that that made him seem so hard? Sienna wondered as the helicopter started to lose height and the dusty brownness of the island rose up to meet them. Among the green and browns she could see the ruins of an ancient temple and wondered to whom it had been built, what deity had commanded the hearts and loyalty of these islanders.

As Alexis explained when they were safely down, because Micros was too small and rocky to support a runway he normally travelled to it by yacht, which was berthed in Piraeus, using the helicopter when time was short. A Land Rover was parked to one side of the small, flat piece of ground where they had come down, and Alexis directed her across to it, the sudden sound in the air behind her warning her that the pilot was taking off, and that now she really was on her own.

A bumpy track led from their landing place downwards through gorse and sparse grass which grew among the rocks, the odd olive tree providing a welcome patch of shade from the searing heat of the Aegean sun. They drove past the ruins Sienna had seen from the sky. They had once been a temple to Diana, Alexis told her, but were too small to merit any interest by the authorities. 'Nearly every island in the group boasts something of the sort,' he told her, 'and if you look carefully when we drive through the village you will also see that nearly every house has at least one piece of stone pillaged from the temple.'

The village nestled in a small cove, the houses clustered by the harbour, a tangle of fishing boats bobbing gently on its calm water. 'Fishing, sponge diving, maintaining a few goats and the odd stand of olive trees, that is how the islanders make their living,' Alexis told her as they drove through, their progress witnessed by a group of wide-eyed children and the silent women knitting in the open doorways that gave on to the street.

As the road climbed they passed a church, gleaming white in the hot sun, a landmark against the parched background of brown and dull greens.

'The island only has two roads,' Alexis told her, 'this one which circumnavigates it, and another which crosses it. Most of the land is useless for anything other than goats.'

It certainly was barren, Sienna acceded, glancing at the rocky outcrops and sparse vegetation, but it also possessed a sombre beauty and its setting, in a sea of dense blue, must surely be unrivalled. The road dipped and she glimpsed a beach of soft white sand, and then ahead of them she saw the house, perched above the bay and looking down on it.

Gleaming white and completely plain, the symmetry of the building instantly appealed to her. They drew up outside it and Alexis opened her door and helped her out into the cobbled courtyard, the scent of thyme reaching her from the flower beds surrounding the cobbles. 'The main windows of the house look out to sea,' Alexis told her as he ushered her towards the door. The house looked modern, too modern to have been commissioned by his father, and when she commented on this Alexis agreed.

'Yes, I commissioned it shortly after his death. Sofia had always loved the island, and I decided to build myself a house here large enough for me to work from if necessary so that I could spend the summer holidays with her.'

He pushed open the door and they were in a pleasant square hall tiled for coolness, the richness of their design offset by the stark white walls and modern lighting. Niches set into the walls revealed exquisite pieces of pottery which Sienna vaguely recognised as Japanese, their colours picked out by those of the tiles, and although Alexis didn't say so, she guessed the pottery was antique and extremely valuable. He opened another door, into a large room with windows overlooking the sea. The room was comfortably furnished in muted creams, bold splashes of colour provided by the cushions which echoed the changing colour of the Aegean, modern paintings adorning the walls.

As Sienna stared round her, another door opened and a plump dark-haired woman dressed in black came bustling in, darting them both an apologetic smile.

'Sienna, this is Maria,' Alexis told her, nodding his head as the woman burst into a torrent of Greek. 'She asks you to forgive her for not being here to greet us, but she is preparing my favourite meal.'

That Maria doted on her employer was patently obvious, but Sienna found that she herself was welcomed warmly, and guessed that Maria had been warned by Alexis about her loss of memory.

'Georges will have brought our cases in from the Land Rover, and Maria will unpack for you. If you would like to have a rest before dinner, Maria will show you to our room. I have some work to catch up on.'

He must have, Sienna recognised, remembering how much time he had spent with her at the hospital, smiling her agreement, and a little alarmed by the intensity of her relief when she was free to go with Maria and escape his magnetic presence.

The room Maria took her to was huge, plainly decorated like the other rooms she had seen, but elegant and comfortable. Off it was a bathroom with a huge bath, large enough to accommodate at least two people, and Sienna found herself avoiding both it and the enormous double bed, which seemed to dominate the restful bedroom. Patio doors opened on to a small patio, the ground dropping away beyond it, providing an endless vista of sea and sky.

'You like?' Maria asked proudly, plumping up cotton pillows and pulling back the heavy cream cotton spread. 'For many years we have wanted the *kyrios* to marry,' she added, 'it is not good for a man to have no sons.' Her eyes rested curiously on Sienna's face, and Sienna began to regret that Alexis was not with them.

'We haven't been married very long yet, Maria,' she said awkwardly, feeling as though she had somehow been found wanting.

A little to her surprise Maria chuckled, the black eyes snapping with mirth. 'With a man like the *kyrios* it does not take long, *kyria*,' she told Sienna. 'He is very much a man, that one. He will give you many fine sons. A woman needs sons to take care of her when she grows old. Georges and I have three. All of them work for the *kyrios* in Athens,' she added proudly, 'the *kyrios* pays for all the children on the island to go to school and learn so that they need not become fishermen like their fathers unless they want to.'

It was a side to her husband Sienna hadn't seen, and yet why should she be so surprised to discover this philanthropic side of him? Hadn't he treated her with kindness and consideration ever since she opened her eyes and saw him?

Long after Maria had gone she lay in bed, knowing that her body ached with tiredness but unable to relax enough to sleep, wondering why she should have this continual feeling of apprehension. She was married to a man who could have married anyone, she was pampered, cared for, desired, and yet she wasn't happy!

Eventually she did sleep, waking to find the room in shadow and much cooler now that the sun had gone down. A brief sound from the bathroom caught her attention, a light shining under the door. It opened and Alexis strode into the room, fastening a clean shirt, his torso gleaming darkly in the half light. He came to an abrupt halt when he realised she was awake.

'Did I disturb you? I didn't mean to, but I needed a shave and a change of clothes. Are you feeling up to dinner, or would you prefer to eat in here? Maria will prepare a tray for you if you wish.'

Sienna had a cowardly impulse to say that she was too tired to eat with him, but it wasn't true, and besides, what was the point of putting off what she knew must eventually come? Surely it was better to get it over with as soon as possible.

Alexis had made it clear that he intended to share her bed, there was no denying that the thought appalled her, but who knew? Once she was in his arms perhaps she would feel differently, perhaps she would even remember how it must have once been between them.

Much to her relief he left her to dress alone, and after one or two false moves she found her way to the small dining room overlooking the sea which like the rest of the house was pleasingly and plainly decorated. Maria served their meal, a fish dish which Sienna found tangy and appetising, accepting the glass of wine Alexis proffered, eagerly, then flushing as she saw the sardonic comprehension in his eyes and the amused lift of his eyebrow. 'Dutch courage?' he enquired amiably, but it was enough to make her pulses flutter and her appetite dwindle until she was pushing the moussaka Maria had served after the first course round her plate with a singular lack of enthusiasm, although she managed to drink another glass of wine.

She refused a sweet and watched Alexis eat a generous portion of honey and almond cake, wondering how on earth he managed to keep so lithe and firm. When he suggested they have their coffee in the main salon she agreed, unable to prevent her body from trembling when he got up and helped her from her chair. In the salon she took a chair placed strategically on its own, and saw his mouth twitch, a muscle beating in his jaw as he sat down opposite her on the oatmeal tweed settee. Maria brought the coffee, and Alexis asked Sienna to pour it.

'Would you like some music?' She nodded an assent, adding, 'but I'll have to leave the choice to you. I can't remember what my likes and dislikes were.'

He made no response, simply selecting a record. Beethoven, Sienna recognised, surprised that she should be able to do so, and she leaned back in her chair, letting the music bathe her in peace. She was half asleep when Alexis touched her, his voice curt as he said, 'Why don't you go to bed. I still have some work to finish and it's been a long day for you.'

She didn't demur, but her legs felt boneless as she tried to stand up and she wondered if he sensed how apprehensive and tense she felt.

Alone in the vastness of the bedroom, she stripped quickly and had a shower, unwilling to linger long over her preparations, unwilling for Alexis to walk in and discover her at her most vulnerable.

Maria had unpacked for her, and after examining several drawers she found one containing her nightwear, fine silk nightdresses in soft pastel colours, things she knew instinctively she could never have afforded, all patently new. Alexis had obviously bought them for her, and as she slid into what was little more than a wisp of peach silk she flushed slightly, wondering if he had pictured her body when he bought them. There was a full-length mirror fronting one of the wardrobes and she glanced at herself in it, shocked to see how the fragile silk emphasised the satin gleam of her skin. She was too thin, she thought appraisingly, but her breasts were surprisingly full, and a quiver ran through her body as she remembered how she had felt when Alexis had touched them.

An hour later still lying wide awake between the

fresh cotton sheets she could feel the tension building up inside her. How long was Alexis going to be? And when he did arrive how was she going to react? How could she permit a man who was still virtually a stranger to her, to make love to her and yet how could she plead for more time? Alexis had made his intentions quite clear and in his shoes would she feel any differently.

Her head ached by the time he eventually arrived, so quietly that she only realised he had done by the opening of the door. He didn't speak to her, simply disappearing into the bathroom. She could hear the sound of running water, and after what seemed to be an aeon of time he reappeared, his hair damp, a brief towelling robe covering his body. When he snapped off the bathroom light the room was plunged into darkness, and Sienna held her breath as she heard him moving about. The bed depressed under his weight, she felt his hand on her shoulder and tensed, dreading what must come next, as she heard him say her name, and turned tensely towards him.

'Ah, so you are awake, I'm sorry if I disturbed you.' She brushed against him in the darkness and recoiled when she discovered that he was naked. His lips brushed her forehead, then she was free and he was turning on to his side, his back towards her. 'Sleep well Sienna,' she heard him say, and she realised with an outraged sense of anti-climax that he was not going to make love to her, and worse, that he was already falling asleep, while she was having to cope with feelings ranging from relief to, surprisingly, mortification.

She turned over herself, burying her hot face in the welcome coolness of her pillow, then tensed as she heard him say, 'It's a woman I want, Sienna, not a human sacrifice. Now go to sleep, there's a good girl.'

And childishly, she would much rather he had insisted on making love to her and that the ordeal of it was over and behind her instead of still in front of her.

CHAPTER SIX

SHE woke up late, to discover that she was alone, and that on the table by the patio door there was a thermos of coffee and a basket which she discovered held croissants and apricot preserve. She glanced at her watch, horrified to discover it was gone ten. Alexis, she presumed, was working. He had shown her last night the room he used as his study. Large and masculine, it was fully computerised so that he could be in contact with any one of his offices without having to stir from inside it.

The coffee was hot and delicious, and Sienna drank three cups, eating two of the croissants, and being surprised by her hearty appetite. The patio doors stood open to the morning, the balmy air and heat a languorous pleasure against her skin, tempting her outside. When she was dressed she would walk down to the cove, she promised herself, but when she discovered a bikini in the drawers she changed her mind and decided that she would not only walk down to it, but swim from it as well. Alexis had said it was perfectly safe, and suddenly after so much time spent in hospital she wanted to stretch her body, to feel the muscles and bones work.

She showered quickly, picking up a towel and donning tee-shirt and shorts over the brevity of the bright cerise bikini. It fastened with bows and was far briefer than anything she would ever have chosen herself, and she wondered what had happened to her own clothes that Alexis should have decided to provide her with an entire new wardrobe.

A path led from the patio down towards the cove, and the scent of thyme rose up from the bushes to meet her as she wended her way through the scrubby vegetation.

The beach, when she reached it, was a perfect half-moon of silver sand, edged by turquoise water, so clean and tantalising that she held her breath, half unable to believe that it was real. When she waded into it the water was pleasurably cool, silky against her skin, and so clear that she could easily see down to the bottom. Several yards out the bottom shelved steeply and Sienna turned to float lazily on her back, lulled by the perfect silence of the morning, all the tension draining out of her.

She swam and floated for half an hour, enjoying the soothing stroke of the water against her sunwarmed skin, and then decided reluctantly that she probably ought to go back. No one knew where she was and the sun was much stronger than she was used to. Even so, when she reached the beach and dried herself off quickly with the towel she had brought, she couldn't resist lying down on the sand for a while, drowsily enjoying the warmth of the sun soaking into her skin. Her eyes closed and she settled more comfortably on to her towel, her good intentions forgotten.

'Sienna!' She woke up with a start, disorientated at first, wondering where she was. Alexis was leaning over her, his torso damp, the dark hair plastered to his head and chest. His body was tanned and supple, and Sienna found herself mutely watching the progress of the droplets of moisture running down his chest. He was wearing a very brief pair of swimming trunks and he grimaced faintly as he saw her glancing at them. 'I don't normally bother, but something told me you might not approve.'

Was he saying that she was a prude? It was true she did feel uncomfortable at having him so close to her, but that was nothing to do with any embarrassment at the sight of his near naked body.

'Alexis. . . .' She wanted to ask him more about her past, but he was quite openly studying the soft swell of her breasts above the taut fabric of her bikini, and she shivered as he leaned forward stroking one finger along her skin.

'For such a slender female you're surprisingly voluptuous,' he murmured lazily. He was so close that she could smell the clean, tangy fragrance of his soap. His jaw was beginning to darken already with the shadow of his beard, and close to his eyes, which she had always thought of as simply grey, revealed a darker band of colour close to the iris.

'Sienna. . . .' He murmured her name again, this time not as a question but as something else, and deep down inside her Sienna felt her body's tremulous response.

When he lowered his head she made no move to evade him, closing her eyes when she felt the warm brush of his lips against hers, coaxingly lazy, a tight feeling as though she were holding her breath invading her chest. Her mind spun dizzily away as Alexis deepened the caress, his mouth moving with determination on hers, his hands stroking along her arms without urgency or heat but somehow arousing inside her a response that demanded that she part her mouth under his, her eyes opening in involuntary reaction as she felt his instant response. Above her he looked dark and faintly menacing, his eyes narrowed, the shadows emphasising the taut thrust of his high cheekbones.

'I think we can dispense with this, don't you?' He whispered the words against her mouth, his hands leaving her arms and finding the ties that secured her bikini top. A small moan that could have been either protest or assent left her lips, stifled under the swift upsurge of pleasure the touch of his hands on her naked skin brought to her.

His fingers, so dark against her paler skin, warmed and aroused, and she gave in to the sensation his touch aroused inside her, lifting her hands from the sand, sliding them round his neck and into the darkness of his hair, arching her body beneath him.

'Ah, yes,' Alexis murmured, his eyes slitted with masculine pleasure in her mute surrender, 'this your body remembers, Sienna, even if you don't. And this. . . .' His mouth touched hers lightly and he drew his thumbs against her nipples, causing her to writhe and murmur a fevered protest, her hands against his skull trying to communicate the need she felt to have his mouth on hers. His hands left her breasts and stroked along her body, igniting flames that seemed to burn through her veins, his mouth still teasing her with light, tormenting kisses.

'Alexis. . . .'

'Touch me, Sienna,' he muttered, watching her. She hesitated, then remembered that this man was her husband and that her body would surely remember to please him even if her mind did not, and her hands moved gently along the slope of his shoulders, her eyes fixed hesitantly on him. 'Not like that, as though you're half afraid of me,' he derided, watching her. 'I won't bite, at least not unless I think it's what you want.' His taunting infuriated her, pink colour flushing her cheeks. It was all right for him. He could remember, while she. . . .

'Perhaps you need a little encouragement.' His voice was husky and came from deep within his throat, roughening slightly as his hands moved over her body again, more urgently this time, his mouth tasting the flavour of her skin, his tongue brushing the delicate hollow beneath her ear, his eyes registering her response to his tormenting caress. She wanted to touch him, she wanted to move beneath him and cry out his name, to wind her arms round his neck and arch her body into him. Shadows of her thoughts chased one another across her face, and he saw them all, smiling mockingly at her as his lips continued to explore her soft skin.

'Alexis. . . .' She wanted to protest that things were moving too fast, that she couldn't cope with the sudden explosion of need he generated inside her, but his questing mouth had already found the vulnerable valley between her breasts, and his murmured 'Mmm?' as he nuzzled the perfumed flesh he found there only brought an involuntary gasp of pleasure to her lips. Her eyes were squeezed tightly shut and she opened them and stared down at him. The weight of his body pinned her to the sand, his hair midnight black against her pale skin, his fingers cupping and caressing her breast, her nipples hard and erect beneath his lazy caress.

'Alexis.' He raised his head, his mouth curled into a half smile, his eyes dark and slitted as his glance shifted from her face, to her breasts and the movement of his thumb against its peak. 'Alexis. . . .!' She gasped and trembled as he turned his head and touched the taut nipple gently between his teeth.

A thousand sensations became just one, her eyes closing on a silent moan of pleasure, her body arching yearningly beneath him, her fingers tightening in his hair, prolonging the aching contact of his mouth against her skin. When he released her a dark flush lay along his cheekbones, his eyes a deep smoky grey as he pulled her down against him, holding her the full length of his body, his hands gripping her hips to let her feel his arousal.

She shivered and tensed, then was suddenly filled with an aching flood of desire, his name an incoherent murmur on her lips as she pressed them feverishly against his throat, feeling him swallow tautly and then groan in hungry pleasure.

'See,' she heard him mutter thickly as his hands slid into her hair, her scalp tingling with pleasure at his touch. 'See how much your body wants to feel mine against it, how hungry mine is for the caress of your lips, how everything that you thought impossible and unwanted suddenly becomes all that you could ever desire. You want me.' He said it flatly, almost as though it were a challenge, and Sienna remembered how very virile and male he was and how it must have hurt his pride to know that she couldn't remember him, or the pleasure they had shared.

'Already you ache for this.' His mouth brushed her breast, his hand flat against the slight swell of her stomach and she ached inside. He drew in his breath tautly and she felt his chest expand against her palms, her delicate skin rasped by the roughness of his body hair. 'You want this.' His hands moved to her hips, pulling her against him, 'and this. . . .' he moved slightly away and bent, brushing the softness of her stomach with his mouth.

Reeling, and dismayed with reaction, Sienna could only make inarticulate murmurs of pleasure. Her skin seemed to be composed of a million nerve endings, each one acutely attuned to his touch. When his mouth ceased moving against her skin she felt sharp pangs of deprivation, and when he held her against his body the barriers of their swimming clothes was a physical pain she couldn't endure.

'And now that you know what you want, perhaps you can understand what I want too.' His fingers were on the bows of her bikini bottom and Sienna didn't try to stop him. The soft brush of his fingers against her naked skin was a pleasure and a pain, and she ran her own hands down the length of his body, feeling the hard contraction of muscles against her palms, the smooth sleekness of his skin against her fingertips, warm and vitally alive, responsive to her touch, his mouth hot as he buried it in the scented skin of her throat. He moved, holding her away slightly, and she drew air into her lungs on a ragged gasp, opening her eyes to find his on her, dark, hot with a passion she needed no memory to understand. She lifted towards him automatically, but he pushed her back, and muttered something under his breath, saying softly, 'That's better, now I can feel all of you against me,' as he grasped her hipbones and lowered himself over her. She gasped beneath the intimate contact with his body, then arched wildly beneath him, driven beyond the limits of her self-control as his hands moved over her, stroking and caressing, his lips teasing her with light kisses, denying her the deeper contact she wanted. Her body was all movement, all restless seeking for something she couldn't comprehend, its movements instinctive and unlearned.

'Touch me, Sienna, kiss me. . . .' This time she needed no further urging, her fingers traced the shape of his bones, her mouth hot against the sunbrowned skin, intent on bringing from him the same fevered response he invoked in her. She touched the flat hardness of his nipples with a hesitant tongue and felt the sudden expansion of his chest as he breathed in harshly.

'You're undermining my self-control,' Alexis muttered thickly, 'and badly!' His hands were on her thighs, thumbs circling the soft flesh, a tight coiling feeling growing inside her, a building towards some explosive force that made her moan softly beneath his touch and drew an equally urgent response from him, his hand guiding hers against his body, his voice thick and fevered as he shuddered in open response to the touch of her hand against him, his mouth hard as he took hers in a deep kiss, his hands moving intimately against her body in a caress that took away her breath and left her weak and fluid, aching for the fulfilment of his possession. All her doubts and fears were forgotten as she responded to the encouragement of his mouth and hands against her, echoing his caresses, feeling his body harden in pleasure, the soft sound of the sea against the beach matching the rhythm his body was beginning to teach hers. He kissed her, probing the inner recesses of her mouth, then the soft skin of her throat, the rounded thrust of her breasts, his fingers circling her wrists, pinning them flat to the ground so that she couldn't reach him, couldn't satisfy her anguished desire to touch him in turn as his mouth moved downwards over her body.

'What is it you want?' His eyes glittered darkly between their thick lashes and Sienna moaned huskily, fighting to free her arms.

'I want to touch you and kiss you,' she told him huskily. 'Alexis!' Her wrists were free, and his hands were on her hips, moving lower while his mouth tasted the soft flesh of her thigh, his teeth nipping gently, as she moved against him, her fingers locked in his hair, the full weight of his torso lying against her thighs.

'I want to taste all of you.' His hand dipped between her thighs and she gasped in undeniable arousal, melting beneath his touch, her mind and body concentrated on the pleasure he was giving her and yet which wasn't enough. She wanted to touch him, to arouse him as he was arousing her. She struggled and felt him tense, moving slightly away, his eyes dark and unreadable.

'It's too late to change your mind now, Sienna.' His voice was hard and unfamiliar, his jaw taut, angry colour darkening his skin, and it thrilled her to know how much he wanted her, hands and mouth eager to make reparation for the wrong impression she had given him. She thought she saw surprise shadow his eyes briefly as he felt her touch against him, and wondered if in the past she had perhaps refused him, but quickly dismissed the thought as unlikely. He aroused her so easily and intensely that she couldn't believe she had ever been able to deny him physically. He groaned as her mouth brushed delicately against his stomach, tensing and then writhing hotly against her, as though unable to prevent himself from responding. His skin felt hot and moist beneath her lips, every muscle tightly controlled.

'Damn you, Sienna,' she heard him mutter thickly, 'stop teasing me!' He groaned again and said hoarsely, 'I ache for you, you little witch!' His hands reached for her, pulling her down beneath him, his mouth hot and urgent as it moved against hers, his thighs parting hers with a rough unsteadiness that made her skin shiver in response. He touched her briefly, stroking her receptive flesh, and her body surged eagerly against him, inciting its thrusting possession. She was surprised by the unexpectedness of the brief pain she felt, then dismissed it as unimportant as Alexis moved inside her, and the coiled, tense feeling she had experienced earlier returned, this time more intensified. She ground her hips against him, impelled by some instinct that couldn't be denied, and felt the weight of his chest as he breathed in in a short gasp, his hands on her hips, holding her against him, his mouth hotly demanding on hers as hunger surged inside him, sweeping her with him into a whirlpool of boiling need, her inarticulate cries silenced by his mouth, her body responding fluidly to the rhythmic thrust of his, carrying them both towards the centre of the cyclone that raged inside her.

Her body exploded with pleasure, eddying circles of it, radiating outwards to every nerve ending, heady, singing pleasure that surely she could not possibly have forgotten, nor the fierce exultation of knowing she had satisfied the driving hunger she had aroused in Alexis.

She glanced down at his chest, still rising and

falling hurriedly, her head pillowed against it, her senses still acutely attuned to the scent and feel of him, their bodies still joined in the aftermath of pleasure. Alexis moved, rolled on to his side and pulled her against him. Sweat beaded his skin and Sienna bent forward to taste it with her tongue, wondering why she should feel such heady pleasure in so very small a thing. She wanted to laugh and cry at the same time, to stretch her body in languorous pleasure, to find the words to describe how she felt, her body tinglingly alive from her scalp right down to her toes, which were right now curled into the sand.

She reached out, letting her hand drift along Alexis' body, enthralled by the simple pleasure of just touching him, then she bent her head and slowly followed the line of dark hair arrowing down past his waist, kissing him softly, feeling his breathing returning to normal, her touch full of tenderness and love.

He opened his eyes and watched her. 'What was that for?'

'Because I wanted to. Do you mind?'

He laughed silently, drawing her against him. 'Mind? Why should I? It's a very pleasurable thing to have a woman touch your body the way you were just touching mine.'

'It was my way of saying "thank you".' She looked away from him, suddenly unsure of herself, unsure of his reaction. She didn't know, did she, how she had behaved towards him before, whether he found her inadequate now that he was a stranger to her. He bent towards her, handing her her bikini and pulling on his own trunks. 'If you stay out here much longer you'll get burned. My skin can take it, yours can't.'

Sienna watched him surreptitiously as he dressed. His body was sleek and firm, the muscles moving easily beneath his skin. It took her breath away that she could find pleasure in so simple a thing as merely looking at him.

'Last night. . . .' She glanced at him hesitantly, wondering why now that she was no longer in his arms she should feel so conscious of a gulf between them, a return of her earlier apprehension.

'Last night?' he prompted, reaching for her towel and folding it.

'I thought. . . .'

'You thought I was going to insist on my husbandly "rights"?' Alexis shook his head. 'Last night you were tired, and tense and very much on your guard against me.'

'How did you know I'd be on the beach?'

'I saw you leave from my study window.'

'And you followed me deliberately?'

'Intent on having my evil way with you?' he mocked. 'Is that what you're thinking? I came to make sure you were all right because you'd been gone so long. When I found you lying here, asleep, I decided to see if I could wake the Sleeping Beauty.' He took her hand as they walked across the sand, pulling her against him to kiss her briefly, before they were within sight of the house. 'And now I must get back to work. Dr Theonstanis said you were to rest and not overdo things, so I suggest you go and lie down for a while after lunch.'

'Alexis.' He stopped and looked at her, his eyes narrowed against the sun, small lines fanning out from his eyes.

'Does it worry you that I can't remember how

things were ... with us before the accident?' She had picked a small wildflower and was systematically destroying its petals until he took it from her.

'Does it worry you?'

'Yes,' she said simply. 'How could I forget such an important part of my life? Surely you and my love for you would be the first things I would remember. . . .'

'So you do remember that you love me?'

She hesitated and gave a small frown. 'Yes. . . . How strange—until I said it, I didn't even know.'

'Your body knew,' Alexis murmured. 'Remember I told you it would.'

'Yes, I'm so glad you found me down on the beach,' she added on a whisper. 'Alexis. . . .'

'Mmm?'

She wanted to ask him if he loved her, but the question died unspoken. It seemed juvenile and silly to demand the spoken proof of his feelings for her when he had taken such good care of her. 'Nothing. . . .'

They went direct to their room, Sienna staring at her reflection in the mirror. Was this tousled, flushed woman really herself? Her eyes glowed golden brown, her expression alive, fulfilled, her body flushed and still warm from Alexis' lovemaking. The open sensuality of her own expression made her eyes widen, the languorous secretive look she could see in her eyes belonged to a stranger.

'Sienna!'

'Sorry, did you say something?'

'I suggested that you might want a shower.' Alexis reached out and touched her skin. 'You're covered in sand and salt.'

'Yes, and my hair's all sticky too. Shall I shower first, then I can dry it while you're getting ready?'

Her throat went dry when she saw the expression in his eyes, the tormenting, knowing look that made her skin ripple with anticipated pleasure.

'I thought we might shower together, but perhaps another time. Dr Theonstanis said you weren't to get overtired. You realise you could be carrying my child?'

It was something she hadn't even thought about, but the note she heard in his voice told her that Alexis had no qualms about fatherhood.

'Was I . . . had we. . . .?'

He shook his head decisely. 'No, but that is not to say that this time my seed will not grow inside you.' His hand caressed her stomach, his palm warm against her skin and she swayed slightly towards him, stunned to discover how much she wanted him. Such a wanting surely was only born of terrible deprivation, and yet until this morning she had not even been aware that she could respond to him. What secrets lay behind the barrier of her memory? Cold fingers of despair played against her spine, and she tried to ignore their chilly message, listening instead to Alexis.

'My body found yours very receptive this morning, Sienna—so receptive that I still hunger for you. Shall I tell Maria that we don't want lunch?' He saw her expression and laughed, a small husky sound of satisfaction.

'Yes, it is a tempting thought, isn't it, but I have work to do, and there is still tonight. Tonight will you tremble and pale when I come to you? Will you hold yourself rigid, repulsing my touch?'

Sienna bowed her head on to his shoulder, tears

stinging her eyes quite unexpectedly. 'I didn't know,' was all she could say. 'I didn't know how it would be between us. Oh, Alexis, I wish I could remember! How did we meet? How did we fall in love? I'm just someone ordinary, you're a wealthy man. . . .' Her voice trailed away uncertainly.

'We met in an office, and I knew the moment I saw you I had to have you.'

'And of course I fell in love with you on sight.'

'So you once told me.'

Her memory would return, it must do, surely there must be many memories she had cherished, many moments she had shared with Alexis she would want to remember. She remembered how she had felt when he touched her and knew that she must be right. She would have to be patient. She would remember in time. She must!

CHAPTER SEVEN

'WOULD you like to stroll through the garden before we go to bed?'

They had been listening to Beethoven again, and Sienna had found herself on the verge of sleep once or twice, lulled there by the plentiful meal and the rich wine she had drunk with it.

Now, as she watched Alexis' dark head bent over the stereo system, excitement curled along her veins. She had slept well and deeply when he left her after lunch and had woken late in the afternoon to find that he had finished his work. They had gone for another swim, but this time there was no lovemaking afterwards, and this time also Alexis dispensed with the brief swimming trunks he had worn before.

She had wanted him to make love to her, she acknowledged, just as she wanted him to now, but instead she agreed that it would be pleasant to walk outside and let him guide her through the patio windows, along one of the narrow gravel paths. The scents of the garden, intensified in the darkness, rose up around them, her own senses intensified also. The warmth of Alexis' hand against her arm sent pleasurable shivers along her spine, and anticipation curled through the pit of her stomach. Her pulses raced hectically and her body felt fluid and boneless. She stumbled on an unseen stone and Alexis caught her, his fingers digging into her waist as he supported her, his breath fanning warmly across her skin. She closed her eyes, breathing in the male scent of him, impelled to lean forward and press her lips against his throat. His silk shirt was open at the neck and beneath her palm she felt his heart begin to pound, his fingers caressing her spine, holding her against him, his throat arching against her lips, his body hard, wanting her.

'Cristos,' he muttered unsteadily, slowly releasing her, 'do you want me to take you here? Now, in the garden, like some impatient boy, aching for his first woman? Perhaps I would have been wiser to leave you untouched, unaware of the desire I can see shining in your eyes.'

Her hunger for him was something that surprised Sienna. They were married, had been lovers, so why should she feel as though she must snatch greedily at the pleasure he offered, why must she have this constant sense of a shadow hanging over them, of doing something vaguely wrong whenever she touched him? Thrusting it aside, she reached towards him, feathering his lips in a teasing kiss, fitting her hips to the masculine thrust of his, expelling her breath on a faint sigh as his control broke and he reached for her, kissing her with hard hunger, the rough fabric of his jeans rubbing against the soft silk of her dress, his body throbbing its hotly urgent message against her.

Her dress had a soft shirt neckline with tiny pearl buttons and he wrenched a few open, bending his head, stroking his tongue along the hollow between her breasts.

'Why in damnation are you wearing a bra?' he protested when his fingers encountered its barrier. 'Your breasts are so perfect you don't need one.' He tugged at the fragile silk satin of her underwear until her breast escaped its confines, his tongue

probing the outline of her already taut nipple over
the fabric of her dress, tormenting them both as
her body thrust against the constraining silk,
anxious for the touch of his mouth.

'I want you.' He said it abruptly, as though for
some reason it angered him, and Sienna turned in
silence and walked with him back to the privacy of
their room. She wanted him too, impatiently,
hungrily, with a need that seemed to have no end
and which was impatient of their clothes, of the
constraints between them, her whispered sighs
melting against his skin as he undressed her
impatiently, her palms already flat to his naked
chest, her mouth exploring the salt moistness of
his skin.

This time there was no long, subtle loveplay,
just a pounding, fierce need which seemed to
overwhelm them both. Sienna met the thrusting
urgency of his body eagerly, her fingernails raking
the taut skin of his back, her teeth biting at his
skin, her head thrown back against his arm, her
body enticing him to take his pleasure of it. The
words he muttered against her increased her
desire, her body arching and pleading, his torso
gleaming softly in the lamplit room as he raised
himself on his forearms, sweat slick skin damp
against her palms as he cried out his pleasure, his
voice fiercely exultant, her own cries lost as he
covered her with his body, his mouth draining the
sweetness from hers, his pleasure hers as he
surrendered to her, lost himself in her and took her
to that same high plateau she had found that
afternoon before they both lifted and soared
through space, falling gently back down to earth.

They slept and made love again, this time more
leisurely, and again Sienna was amazed at the

depth of her own response, as the pleasure she found in just touching and tasting the masculinity of him. Her own abandonment to his caresses was something else that surprised her. She had checked once as he touched her intimately his mouth against her thigh, but he had overruled her opposition and she had given way wantonly to the waves of pleasure he was drawing from her body, giving herself up completely to the languorous delight spreading through her.

When she woke again Alexis was still asleep. She was lying curled against his body and she touched it gently, mutely adoring his masculine contours. He stirred in his sleep and murmured something indecipherable, his hand moving along her arm to find and possess her breast. She felt fluid, formless, rough clay from which he could fashion her into anything he might choose, she gloried in the responsiveness of her body to his touch, and yet was aware that it left her defenceless in a way that he would never be.

He woke up, dark eyes instantly alert, a wicked smile curling the corners of his mouth. 'Alexis. . . .' He waited for her question, stroking the taut aureole of her nipple slowly, so that pleasure uncurled inside her and she wanted to twine herself around him, but she held back, and asked uncertainly, 'Were you . . . were you my first lover, or. . . .'

'First, and last,' he told her brusquely. His thumb ceased its arousing movement and she felt him withdraw from her. 'You were no wanton, if that's what troubles you.'

'It frightens me that I can be so responsive to you and yet not know you.'

'Your body knows me,' he reminded her. 'It is only your mind that has forgotten.'

'You must have known many women.'

'Very many,' he agreed sardonically. 'What is it you wish to ask me, Sienna? If I find you more desirable than I did them? You are my wife, surely that answers your question, even if my body does not. Are you going to swim with me this morning? If so, I suggest that we can dispense with your bikini. I should like to feel your body slide against mine beneath the water, soft and cool, your eyes darkening to desire as I touch you, your body welcoming mine.'

He had started to kiss her, brief tormenting kisses that made her clutch at his shoulders, and arch against him until she felt him tense and lift his head. She saw that he was listening to something and listened too.

'Helicopter,' he said tersely. 'I'd better get dressed and see who it is. You stay here.'

He was gone before she could protest, striding naked into the bathroom, his skin tanned evenly all over, the faint marks on his body where her teeth had touched him in passion, bringing a flush of colour to her face as she remembered the total abandon of their lovemaking the previous night. He had incited her to do things she had never imagined herself wanting to do, and she tensed, suddenly puzzled to know how she had known that fact, how she had known what her thoughts and feelings had been in the life she lived prior to her accident.

When Alexis re-emerged his hair was damp, his skin dark and taut against the white towel he had wrapped round his hips. He got dressed quickly, jeans and a soft white cotton shirt. Sienna watched him tuck it into his pants and felt a spiral of pleasure rising inside her. Just to look at him made her ache.

'I shouldn't be too long. It's probably someone bringing me some papers.'

When he was gone she lay staring at the ceiling and then, suddenly impatient and restless, she got up. The bathroom still smelled of his soap and she closed her eyes beneat the sting of the shower, imagining that he was with her, her body tensing and her breasts swelling slightly with need.

She dressed quickly in pale pink jeans and a toning tee-shirt. Her skin still held a flush from yesterday's sun and her blonde hair curled softly on to her shoulders. She moisturised her face, and applied a soft taupe eyeshadow and a slick of lip gloss. Her mouth was swollen, not enough to be painful, but enough to let anyone who looked at her know that she had been passionately kissed. She touched her mouth wonderingly, her eyes unknowingly languorous, then shook herself, half shocked by the direction of her thoughts.

She could hear Alexis speaking as she approached the salon. He sounded angry, his voice terse and hard. 'You know I asked you not to come here,' she heard him say, and then a woman's voice responded unhappily, 'But, Alexis, I had to—when I heard what you had done. *Cristos*, how could you have done such a thing! Alexis, I cannot believe it of you!'

A knife twisted white-hot fire in Sienna's heart and she crept to the door. Who was Alexis talking to? Not someone who had brought him any papers, important or otherwise, she was sure of that. No, it was another woman in there with him, a woman who like her had perhaps known the delight of his lovemaking, who didn't want to step aside for a mere wife. She looked at the door. It was slightly open and all at once she was

consumed by a need to see her rival. She
approached the door silently and looked through
it—and the colour drained from her face, a
shocked moan leaving her lips, she must have
touched the door, because it swung open and she
saw Alexis turn and then stare at her, his face hard
and angry. The girl talking to him was watching
her too, and Sienna shivered. Dear God, what a
fool she had been! A lover! This dark-haired girl
with the anxious eyes and pale skin was no lover.
She held out her hand, her head high, her eyes
blazing hatred and bitterness at Alexis, and said
calmly, 'Hello, Sofia.'

A look passed between brother and sister, and
correctly interpreting it, Sienna said brittlely, 'Yes,
amazing, isn't it? I heard voices and thought I had
discovered my husband with another woman.
Until I saw you.'

'Sienna!' Alexis spoke hoarsely and she looked at
him, and on a sudden juddering stab of memory
heard his voice saying her name, the sound
echoing down long canyons of pain and humiliation, her own voice responding as though it were
part of a prayer. 'I love you . . . I love you. . . .'

Alexis was watching her and said slowly,
'You've remembered, haven't you?'

'Everything.' Was that really her voice, so light
and brittle? 'How very piquant you must have
found it, having me here ignorant of everything that
happened between us, not able to understand why
I should feel that it was "wrong" for us to make
love!' Her face twisted, mirroring the pain she
could feel wrenching inside her, goading her on
despite Alexis' angry, hard face, and Sofia's
shocked, disturbed one.

'*You* understood didn't you, Alexis, but that

didn't stop you. But then, of course, I gave you the ideal opportunity to take a little more revenge, didn't I? I've heard it's like salt water, the more you drink the more you need.'

'Sienna, let me explain.'

'Explain what? There is nothing to explain. I already know it all.

'I made a mistake,' Alexis said quietly. 'Am I to be condemned for the rest of my life for that?'

'A mistake!' Through her pain Sienna stared at him bitterly, wondering if he really knew what he had done. He had destroyed and dissected her emotions, reducing her to the status of a foolish adolescent, easily bemused by the sensual expertise of an experienced man, but there was more to it than that. She had loved him from that first brief sight of him, had loved him without knowing him, without being aware of who he was, had recognised him as a man she would love, giving herself over completely to him. That very first day he could have taken her hand and led her anywhere, her commitment to him was as basic and deep-rooted as that, and that he had failed to perceive it was her only hope of salvation because it showed her that he was not the man she had thought him to be. She had thought herself free of her love for him, but he had used her amnesia, just as he had used her. . . .

She turned and ran from the room in much the same way as she had done on that other occasion, again half blinded by tears, the cruel grip of Alexis' fingers in her arm detaining her. She fought against him like a wild thing, conscious of Sofia's unhappy face, of Alexis' cruelly implacable one, of Maria suddenly appearing from out of nowhere, of Alexis hitting her briefly with his open palm, and then picking up her broken body, carrying her towards their room. The last place on earth she wanted to be!

She struggled in his arms, crying out that she would not go back there, but he ignored her, thrusting open the door and dropping her on to the bed. He held her throat while he forced her to take two tablets and a glass of water, then watched as she fought them for endless minutes, his scrutiny as pitiless and cold as she remembered it from that night at the cottage.

She tried to keep awake, but the pills were too strong for her and she felt her senses slide impotently away, then Alexis was pushing her down against the bed, covering her with the cotton spread, then going to stand by the door, his expression unfathomable as he looked towards her, darkness reaching up to enfold her in its heavy embrace, someone she didn't realise was herself crying like a lonely child, the sound dying gradually as she gave herself up to oblivion.

When she woke up he was standing by the bed, watching her, his eyes empty of all expression, arms folded across his chest. Sienna breathed in deeply, feeling the pain inside her grow. She turned away so that he couldn't see the tears threatening to fall. Her glance fell on the clock beside the bed, and she frowned. Nine? But it had been just after lunch when he gave her those tablets, and now it was broad daylight. She had almost slept the clock round!

'Where's Sofia?' How odd that she should ask that question when so many far more important ones clamoured for answers.

'Gone. I sent her back to Athens.'

'That's a pity.' How toneless and light her voice

sounded, stripped of all emotion and feeling. She blinked back the tears which had threatened earlier, now under control, her face carefully blank. Alexis moved and she saw the echoing ripple of muscles beneath his shirt, her stomach clenching against a wave of self-loathing as she remembered how she had touched him, revealed her most intimate thoughts to him, loved him, and all the time. . . . 'How long will it take to get a helicopter here?' she asked in that same bright dead voice. 'I'd like to leave as soon as possible. I. . . .'

'You're not leaving. How much exactly have you remembered?' His voice was as empty as her own, but when he turned into the light she could see faint lines of what might have been strain etched against his skin.

'Everything. All of it—how we met, how you made love to me because you thought Rob had raped Sofia. How could you do this to me, Alexis?' she demanded, her control suddenly breaking. 'How could you bring me here, knowing? How could you have married me?' A fresh thought struck her. 'Are we married, or is that just another game you're playing, another. . . .'

'Stop this—you're becoming hysterical, Sienna! Believe me,' he added darkly, 'no one regrets what has happened more than me, but it has happened. Because of me you came dangerously close to losing your life. We are married,' he told her curtly, his expression grim when he saw the disbelief in her face. 'You said yourself you remembered the ceremony. It took place at the hospital. It was relatively easy to organise once they knew the circumstances.'

'What did you tell them?' She was bitterly angry, more angry than she had been even when he told her that he didn't love her, that he simply wanted revenge. He had come close to destroying her life once and she had thought herself free of him, but humilating her once apparently wasn't enough for him, he had wanted to repeat the experience.

'I told them that we were engaged, that you could be carrying my child, that marriage was what we both wanted. You were in a coma for several days after the accident. They thought at one point that they might have to operate. Your brother couldn't be reached, and they agreed to the marriage because they knew that as your husband I would have the authority to give them permission to operate should it be needed.'

'But why?' Sienna demanded bitterly. 'Why marriage? Why. . . .'

'I am Greek.' Alexis reminded her curtly. 'My family has a code of honour that goes back to the dawn of our time. I had dishonoured you, it was my fault that the accident occurred. The only reparation I could make was the protection of my name.' His mouth was wry. 'If you are honest with yourself it was, after all, what you wanted.'

'No!' Sienna was so angry that she threw the denial at him violently. 'What I wanted was the man I thought loved me as I loved him, the man I foolishly trusted, a man you taught me simply does not exist, Alexis. I should have listened more carefully to what my mind was trying to tell me when I was in hospital. No wonder I felt so apprehensive, so doubtful about you! You lied to me, Alexis. You knew I would never have left Athens with you had I known the truth. You let me think we'd been married for some time, that our marriage was completely normal!'

'Rest assured that it will be,' he told her grimly. 'We are married, Sienna, that is an incontrovertible fact, and our marriage will stand. It has, after all, been consumated.'

She went red and then white, her voice a husky rustle of pain as she whispered, 'Because you tricked me. You knew that inwardly I doubted you, that it was only because I thought the blame for not remembering you lay with me, because I thought I was the one cheating you.' Her voice broke and she laughed wildly, 'You knew all that and yet you let me. . . .' Love you, she had been about to say, but she closed her mouth in a hard line over the words. No wonder she had felt that starving need for him, that hunger to take and keep on taking, storing up her memories. Her mind had known even then that she was living in a fool's paradise. 'I think I could forgive you all the rest, but that, that is something I could never forgive.'

Alexis' voice, in direct opposition to hers, was flat, completely devoid of any interpretable emotion. 'By "that" I assume you are referring to our lovemaking? Whether I had told you the facts or not wouldn't have made any difference, Sienna. We would still have made love. I knew that first night at the cottage that sexually we were extremely compatible.' A small smile curved his mouth, but it was a cold assessing gesture. 'Remember then how you told me "next time". . . .'

'Yes.' Her face was hot, her voice terse and bitter. 'And you told me there never would be a "next time", that I would never find pleasure in your arms.'

He shrugged carelessly. 'So I was wrong, on

both counts.' He crossed the floor swiftly, grasping her chin before she could turn away, his breath warm against her skin, his eyes dark and angry, as he forced her to meet them. 'You can't deny that you responded to me, Sienna, that you wanted me, that. . . .'

'That I was living a lie,' Sienna said angrily, 'But I can't live it any longer now that I know the truth. I can't live with you as your wife now, Alexis, you must see that.'

'No,' he said evenly, 'I don't see it. What is the difference between then and now? Will your body react differently to mine because you know the truth?' he said savagely, anger flaring deeply in his eyes. 'What is the difference?'

'The difference is in knowing that . . . that there is no love between us,' Sienna told him thickly, 'in knowing that you married me because you felt you had to . . . because it was your "duty".'

'And because of that you would condemn us both, deny us both the pleasure you know full well we find in one another?'

'I only found that pleasure because I thought we loved one another,' Sienna said hotly. 'Do you honestly believe that a woman who ran from you as I did would find "pleasure", as you call it, in your touch?'

His mouth was sardonic. 'You might very well *find it*, but no, I don't suppose you would admit to it. The very fact that you did run proves to me that you aren't indifferent to me, Sienna. You once told me you loved me, now you claim to hate me, both powerful emotions which cannot be easily subdued.'

'I loved the man I thought you were,' Sienna cried out passionately, 'and I hate the man I now know you to be. This marriage must end, Alexis. I can't live with you now, knowing the truth, and I won't!'

'We are married and we shall stay married. There has never been a divorce in my family, and I am not going to be the first.'

She knew it was useless to continue arguing with him in his present frame of mind. Here on the island she was virtually his prisoner if he chose to make her so, and she contented herself with an acid, 'Very well, if you say so, but I shall never live with you again as your wife.'

His mouth curled, something dark and unnamable leaping to life in his eyes, making her shrink back against her pillows, her pulses thudding out warning messages to her brain. 'Then I must just pray that you are already carrying my son, otherwise. . . .'

'Otherwise you'll do what?' Sienna taunted, not heeding the messages from her brain. 'Rape me, as you once accused my brother of raping your sister? Dear God, it only needs that, doesn't it, to complete this farce full circle! Please leave me now, Alexis,' she finished tiredly. 'What would you have done if Sofia hadn't arrived when she did?' she asked as he walked towards the door. 'Gone on letting me live in a pretence world, keeping me here so that I would never remember the truth?'

'I didn't tell you because Dr Theonstanis said it was best if you remembered the past naturally, and your reaction proves the truth of his advice. You are behaving more like an hysterical child than a woman, Sienna. You once said you loved me, but it is a poor kind of love that will not allow the beloved to make any mistakes, that sets him up on a pedestal and condemns him to remain there. We are married and our marriage cannot be set aside. I admired your bravery in defending your brother and in protecting him by not telling him what had happened, and I would have been pleased to have such a woman as the mother of my sons, but like you I begin to believe I was deceived, because I have seen no evidence of her this morning. Why cannot you be honest and admit that we could build a life together on what we have?'

'What we have? You mean sex!' Sienna said it disparagingly, and wished she hadn't when she saw the dark colour seeping up under his skin. He was angry and it showed in the clenched muscles of his face, the hot glitter of his eyes as they raked her pale features.

'How easily and lightly you dismiss it, but you will not find it so easy to dismiss for very long, Sienna. There will come a time when your body will cry out for mine, when you will lie awake remembering how it was between us, when you want the touch of my lips against your skin, my body against yours, when you will yearn to toss aside pride and anger to come to me.'

'Never!'

His mouth hardened. 'I am not prepared to bandy words with you any longer. When you have decided to revert to adulthood once more we can talk. Until then I shall leave you to sulk alone.'

'I suppose I'm allowed to write to Rob? When he gets back he'll wonder what's happened to me and where I am.'

'Of course you may write to your brother. He is also quite welcome to visit us here whenever he wishes—but bear this in mind, Sienna, I will not have you confiding the secrets of our marriage to anyone—do I make myself clear?'

She wanted to demand to know by what means he would enforce his threat, then she remembered Rob's face when he said he himself would probably want to kill any man who harmed her. If she told Rob the truth she would be exposing him to possible danger. As Rob himself had told her, Alexis was rich and powerful enough to destroy her brother, and she knew that for Rob's sake, on this occasion she could not pour out her troubles to him, and that Alexis had won that point if no other.

'At least I suppose I have the consolation of knowing I married a rich man,' she said disdainfully as Alexis opened the door. She threw the taunt at him, wanting to find his Achilles heel, wanting to make him suffer as she was suffering.

He paused, then said tiredly without turning, 'It won't work, Sienna. You forget I know more about you than you know about yourself. Wealth and possessions mean very little to you.'

He was gone, and she was alone with the torment of her thoughts, images which she had kept at bay ever since she opened the door and saw Sofia and the past came rushing back to her, making her eyes ache with unshed tears and her heart sore with pain. Alexis had married her because his pride demanded it, because he had discovered the truth. Once marriage to Alexis had been all that she had desired in the world, but it was a hollow fulfilment she had now. She had wanted the Alexis she believed loved her, and she shuddered in self-loathing, remembering how she had responded to the touch of his hands, the brush of his mouth over sensitive skin, the way she had kissed and caressed him, every gesture a betrayal of her most intimate thoughts and feelings. She had believed that there was love between them and had given herself to him in the security of that love, and he had let her. That was what she couldn't forgive—he had knowingly let her make a fool of herself twice over. He could have stopped her. He could have told her their marriage had been an arranged one—there were any number of ways a man of his experience and astuteness could have controlled the tempo of their relationship so that she hadn't abandoned herself to him so thoroughly, but he had not done so

How he must have laughed at her in secret, delighting in her unwitting self-betrayal, knowing all the time that had she not forgotten the past she would never have let him come within a mile of her. Had it added piquancy, excitement, relish perhaps to his response to her knowing the truth? No doubt he had been amused by the adoration she had showered on him, the delight she had shown in finding herself so responsive to him, the awe he kindled inside her when he made love to her. Dear God, how was she going to stand it? How could she endure living alongside him with the knowledge of her own humiliation?

She would have to find a way. But she intended to make it clear to Alexis that she would never again share his bed. Never. She gritted her teeth. Never, never, never would he hear her say she wanted him, never again would she turn to him, her voice soft with longing, her body warm and pliant. So complete had been her self-betrayal, her unwitting self humiliation, her loss of pride and self-respect that self-loathing lived inside her like a sickness, and the only cure for it would be the knowledge that where Alexis was concerned she was completely invincible. She would rather die than turn to him in need and hunger, rather face the very worst form of physical torture than have to face her own reflection in the mirror if she ever proved him right when he claimed that she would want him.

For days they lived as strangers, coolly polite when they met, with Sienna taking care that it was infrequently. The villa had several guest rooms and she had moved into one of them, braving Maria's disapproving and concerned clucks, ignoring the tightness of Alexis' mouth when he discovered what she had done. No doubt he still believed that her need of the physical fulfilment they had shared would bring her back to his bed, humbled and grateful for whatever he might give her, but he was wrong.

She spent her days exploring the island on foot, keeping sedulously away from the bay where she had swum that first morning and where later Alexis had tricked her into betraying herself.

She borrowed the Land Rover and drove into the village huddled by the harbour, delighting the inhabitants with her slow Greek, examining the muddled array of goods in the one general store the village boasted. While she explored, Alexis worked. Whenever she walked past his study she could hear the hum of computer equipment, but she never ventured inside. A son, Alexis had told her, that was what he wanted from her, but she already knew that there would be no child. It was something she wouldn't be able to keep from Alexis for ever, and what would happen when he eventually learned the truth? Her stomach nerves tightened in apprehension. If he insisted that she conceive his son, he would get no assistance from her! It wouldn't be a woman he held in his arms but a piece of wood. She had no illusions left. He was hard and determined enough to take her anyway, and she was not naïve enough to believe that he would deny himself for her sake, after all he had already quite deliberately allowed her to give to him and to give generously and lovingly all that she had to give, all the time knowing that he could never match or share her feelings, and that ultimately she would suffer because of him.

CHAPTER EIGHT

'I HAVE to go to Athens. The helicopter will be here in half an hour, would you like to come with me?'

'You mean you're actually willing to allow me off my leash? How trusting of you!' Sienna mocked, putting down her cup of coffee and studying Alexis' face with coolly mocking eyes. It had been like this for the past few days, ever since she had realised that she wasn't carrying his child, and Alexis, surprisingly, had let her continue to draw blood, and claw him with her acid comments, her perpetual enforcement of the fact that she loathed him.

'What could you do? You have no money, no passport, and for some reason of your own, pride perhaps, I know you will not appeal to your brother.'

He was astute, Sienna had to acknowledge that. She had written to Rob simply telling him that they were married. She had mentioned their meeting at the Savoy as though it had been the first, and hoped he wouldn't compare notes with Gill. A whirlwind affair, she had called it, trying to make her letter sound happy and lighthearted as though it really had come from a new bride still very much in love with her husband. No, she would never tell Alexis why she couldn't tell Rob the truth. It would only give him another hold over her, and one she guessed he would not hesitate to use. Although he had said nothing when she taunted him she had seen deep in his eyes

138

the smouldering anger he was keeping banked
down, and sensed that it was dangerous.

'Do you wish to come with me, Sienna, or not?'

'Not,' she said with a cool smile. 'After all, if I
come with you it means I shall have to spend time
in your company, if I don't, I shall be free of you
for as long as you stay away. I'm really surprised
you needed to ask.'

'You can't keep this up indefinitely, Sienna.' His
voice was hard with warning. 'You are not a child,
for all that you seem to be delighting in behaving
like one at the moment. We are married. Nothing
can alter that fact.'

'We are married because you chose to marry me,'
Sienna pointed out, her mouth curling disdainfully,
'I wasn't given any choice in the matter.'

'No, but it isn't our marriage that is responsible
for this . . . this childish display of resentment, is it,
Sienna? It is because I made love to you and you
enjoyed it.'

Her face went white, and she pushed back her
chair, springing up from the table, tensing as
Alexis reached out to grasp her wrists and
imprison her against the hard wooden edge as he
stood up. Trapped between the table and the
hardness of Alexis' thighs, she went perfectly still,
breathing tormentedly, acutely conscious of the
rough brush of his denim-clad thigh against the
tanned bareness of her legs in the brief shorts and
tee-shirt she had donned for her after-breakfast
walk. He was deliberately imposing himself on her
senses, compelling her body's attention to his
proximity, telling her without words that he had
the power to dominate her, and the knowledge
seemed to release some powerful drug inside her
which heated her blood and roused her temper.

'What are you going to do?' she demanded huskily, refusing to be quelled by his proximity. 'Force me to accept your body because you know *I* will no longer do so willingly?'

'Force you?' His eyebrows drew together, his thumbs stroking the inner flesh of her wrists, 'Oh no, Sienna, I won't be caught in that trap. You *want* me to force you,' he told her bluntly, 'You want me to prove you right and give you a real reason for all this supposed "hatred". If you want to play games go right ahead, I'm not going to stop you, but I'm not going to join you either.' He bent his head, and captured her startled mouth, silencing her words, kissing her with a slow sweetness, taking his time over his exploration of her mouth, before he finally released her.

'Something to think about while I'm gone,' he told her softly, as he stepped back. 'Something to take to bed with you and think about when you feel lonely.'

'*My* bed isn't lonely, Alexis,' she assured him crisply, 'even if yours is.'

'Was,' he murmured trenchantly, and she knew without another word having to be said that one of the reasons he was going to Athens was because he had a woman there, a woman who would no doubt be only too glad to share his sensual expertise, and she shuddered deeply, closing her eyes for a second, hating him with every pulsating nerve of her body. When she opened her eyes she was alone and he had gone. She went upstairs to her room, playing idly with her make-up and making a pretence of sorting through her wardrobe, emerging only when she had heard the helicopter land and then take off again.

Strangely, Alexis' departure left her feeling

restless, her intended walk suddenly unappealing. She found Maria in the kitchen and told her she was going out, guessing that Maria disapproved of her remaining behind while Alexis was in Athens.

Perhaps she should have gone with him. She could have at least done some sightseeing. She bit her lip in vexation, halting suddenly as she realised that Alexis might never have intended to take her with him and that his invitation might have been tendered in the sure knowledge that she would refuse it. In her heart of hearts she knew things could not continue as they were. Behaving the way she was doing was something that did not come easily to her, and only her determination to make Alexis see the impossibility of their marriage continuing kept her going, her initial bitterness had started to fade and the logic she had learned from her father reasserted itself. Perhaps Alexis had felt that by marrying her he was doing the right thing, and she could well understand why he had chosen not to encourage her to regain her memory. Perhaps even he was right when he claimed, as he had done in a fit of anger one evening, that if she had regained her memory twelve months after the accident she would not have behaved, as he termed it, 'like a petulant child'.

With twelve months of living as his wife behind her would her sense of betrayal, of having been deceived have been tempered by the fact that they had established a life together? Surely no matter when she had remembered there would always be this terrible hurt and anger inside her. Not because he had married her but . . . but because of the way he had made love to her, an inner voice whispered, because he had taught her such pleasure and joy and she had responded to him in eager innocence, and he had let her. Never once had he tried to stem the words of love she murmured against his skin, never once had he checked her when she expressed by touch and speech how she felt about him, and yet he had known, *must* have known, that she would have died rather than utter one word, offer one caress that might have betrayed her, after the way he had treated her at the cottage.

Whenever she thought about her response to him, her adoration of his body, she writhed in a torment of self-loathing, wishing it was possible to blot the memories out of her mind—just as she had blotted *Alexis* out of her mind? Because that was what she had done. Had they quarrelled? she had asked Alexis uncertainly. Why should she have forgotten him, her husband, her lover? and he ... he had not said one single word which might have pointed her in the right direction but instead had let her wander among a potential minefield of emotions callously letting her take the path he must have known would lead to self-destruction. And yet, she remembered that he had looked angry whenever she said that she couldn't remember him, and she had thought it because his pride was hurt, because he loved her and she couldn't remember that loving.

He had been gone three days when she finally admitted to herself that she missed him. She missed their abrasive conversations, the glimpses of his dark head as he studied the papers he seemed to bring with him to every meal now, the acerbic exchanges between them which had taken the place of the physical communication they had shared when he first brought her to the island. She missed him and she loved him.

She shuddered as the truth she had fought so long to conceal refused to remain submerged, surfacing past all the barriers she had used to hold it down, forcing itself upon her mind, making her accept its reality. She loved Alexis. How could she have ever imagined that love was something she could take back simply because she found that the recipient did not treasure it as she had hoped? So where did that leave her? It left her married to a man she loved, but who did not love her, a man, moreover, who would not hesitate to trade on her feelings for him should it suit him to do so. As she saw it she had two alternatives—stay and run the risk of Alexis eventually discovering the truth and using it against her, or leave. But Alexis would not allow her to leave. She gnawed at her bottom lip, worrying at the problem. She could not be happy married to Alexis, forced to live off the crumbs of affection he threw to her when he thought the need arose, bearing his children, being his wife, but not having his love. It would cripple her emotionally and surely foster in him only contempt for her. That meant she must leave. But if she tried, Alexis would bring her back. Unless of course he asked her to leave, wanted her to go. The pain that thought brought her was nothing worse than that she had experienced when she discovered he didn't love her, she told herself stoically, it could be endured, she would endure it and she would find a way to make Alexis send her away. She had to.

The third evening of his absence she left her dinner after only a few mouthfuls. Maria clucked impatiently when she saw her plate, frowning over it and shaking her head. 'Is not good that you do not eat. The *kyrios* would not approve.'

'I'm just not very hungry, Maria,' Sienna told

her, proffering a conciliatory smile. 'Time you make a baby, then you are hungry,' Maria told her forthrightly. 'The *kyrios* needs sons. All men need sons.'

Yes, Alexis wanted children, and perhaps that might be his Achilles heel. Sienna got up from the table and walked out into the garden. The scent from the flower beds reached out to embrace her, and tears stung her eyes as she remembered the first time she had walked in these gardens with Alexis. How eagerly she had gone with him, how eagerly she had turned to him, her bones turned fluid by his voice, his touch. She had angered him by refusing to sleep with him, her resistance infuriating him all the more because he knew how much she wanted him.

'You will want me,' he had said to her, and she did, and it shamed her to her soul that she should. His lovemaking seemed to have the same effect on her as a potent drug. She wanted his touch, craved and hungered for it, and if he hadn't been away, she didn't know if she would have been equal to the struggle of preventing herself from abasing herself in front of him and pleading for it, as he had told her she would. But no, she would not permit herself that final humiliation. The same pride which had helped her to endure the truth on that first occasion came to her rescue now, and she made a mental vow that no matter what happened she would never again go to Alexis voluntarily, no matter how much she might want to.

She walked further than she intended, so wrapped up in her thoughts that it was a shock to discover she had wandered down to the small bay below the house. A cool breeze blew in off the Aegean—a warning of a *meltimi* wind to come?

Sienna shivered as she gazed out over Homer's 'wine-dark' seas, thinking how aptly he had named them, wondering what Alexis was doing, whom he was with. She was only wearing a thin tee-shirt and skirt and the breeze was cold enough to raise goose pimples on her skin. Nevertheless, she paused for a moment staring out to sea, reluctant to return to the loneliness of the villa, the emptiness all around her without Alexis.

Eventually she moved slowly back towards the path, wrapping her arms round her cold body, and shivering slightly as she increased her walking pace. It was still only early, perhaps she would listen to some music, or read a book, both had been favourite pastimes, but now they palled, now everything that wasn't Alexis palled, she admitted to herself.

She had nearly reached the patio when the shadow detached itself from the vines of the bougainvillaea where they climbed along the wall, and moved towards her, dark and faintly menacing, her breath catching in her throat until the moon slid from behind a cloud and revealed to her the features of her husband. He was dressed casually in jeans and a fine cotton shirt, the sleeves rolled up and the throat unbuttoned so that she could see the dark fine hair growing there.

'Alexis.' Her hand crept to her own throat, instinctively covering the hurried thud of her pulse. Suddenly it was very difficult to breathe, the ebb and flow of the blood through her veins a physical reality that echoed her uneven heartbeat. 'You startled me—I didn't know you were back. I never heard the helicopter.'

'I didn't use it, I brought the yacht. It's anchored in the harbour.'

She made to step past him, intensely aware of his proximity, of the scent and shape of his body, both somehow heightened by the enfolding darkness. The room behind him was illuminated with a single lamp, throwing out soft shadows, creating an aura of intimacy that threatened to choke her.

'I think I'll go in. I stayed out longer than I intended, and it's gone quite cool.'

'Hardly a warm welcome,' Alexis jeered softly. 'Why are you so tense? What are you frightened of, Sienna?'

'Nothing, I'm just cold and tired.'

'Tired?' His voice mocked her. 'It's only nine o'clock. Why did you stay down in the cove so long if you were cold?' he asked abruptly. Had he known she was in the cove? She frowned, suddenly feeling ill at ease.

'Why not? The sea has a very hypnotic effect.' She tried to move past him and found that he was blocking her way and that in order to move she would have to brush against him. Her body tensed involuntarily at the thought of any contact with him. How could she preserve her supposed indifference if she had to touch him? She knew it would tax her self-control too far. She hesitated and moved away, just too late. Alexis reached out, his fingers brushing her arm.

'You *are* cold.' His voice was rough. 'Here, put this on.' He reached behind him to one of the white patio chairs and gave her a thick woollen jumper. 'It won't bite,' he told her sardonically when she shrank back, cursing suddenly as she stepped off the edge of the patio and stumbled backward. His hands reached for her as hers came to fend him off, gripping her round the waist, spinning her round until her face was in the light from the lamplit room and his was in the shadow. 'Am I so terrifying that you would rather break your ankle than permit me to touch you?' he demanded harshly, 'or is it me you are frightened of, Sienna?'

'I'm not frightened.' How unsteady her voice sounded, how different from the calm, controlled image she wanted to project! She tried to move within his imprisoning grasp, to put a safer distance between herself, and the warm male-scented enticement of his body, but her small hands were useless against the hard muscles of his arms, the flesh and sinew hard beneath her fingertips.

'Please let go of me, Alexis,' she asked huskily.

'Why? Are you perhaps finding you are not as indifferent to me as you have tried to pretend. Are you ready to admit that I was right, that you do still want me? What's the point in pretending? We both know how responsive you are to me.'

Another minute and he would be kissing her, Sienna could sense the powerful tension within him to dominate her to his will, and suddenly she realised that she might have found his Achilles heel and the means by which she could get him to send her away.

'You mean you *think* you know,' she corrected lightly, willing herself not to betray any signs of tremulousness or uncertainty. 'Didn't it ever occur to you that my "responsiveness" might have been faked? I did after all believe you to be my husband, you aren't the only one with a sense of honour and duty, Alexis. I made love with you because I believed you had a right to demand that kind of commitment from me, because I genuinely believed that *we* were in love, even though I could no longer remember that emotion. I thought you cared about me and that you would be hurt by any hint of rejection, just as I would have been hurt had the positions been reversed, had I discovered that the husband I believed loved me had lost his memory and with it all memory of our love. I forced myself to be what I thought you had a right to accept, and because you are a very ... experienced lover my body responded—more out of relief than desire, I'm sure. I was so terrified that you would guess how empty I felt inside. How guilty ...'

'No!' He uttered the denial, harshly. 'No, Sienna, it won't work—you responded to me, you touched me as a woman touches the man she loves and desires above all others.'

'I touched you as I believed you had a right to be touched,' Sienna corrected lightly. 'You must remember that the person I was when we made love never really existed, she wasn't me, Alexis, she could never be me. All of it was only because you were my husband. Because of that and what I felt I owed you I ...'

'You what? Forced yourself to submit to me?'

She could tell even without seeing his face that it was dark with anger, that his eyes were glittering with the force of it, his muscles compacted under the strain of denying it an outlet. A terrible, tearing pain splintered inside her and she wanted to call back the words, to appease his pride, but she could not. For the sake of her own salvation she must not.

'Is that what you're trying to tell me, Sienna?' he demanded through gritted teeth, 'that you forced yourself to endure this?' He bent his head, feathering his lips lightly across hers, warming their cold contours. She felt her heart leap and lodge somewhere in her throat as she withstood the sensual caress. He had himself under control now, the anger banked down under a greater need, but Sienna knew it was still there, waiting to burst into life the moment she put a light to it. 'And this . . .' Alexis murmured against her closed lips, 'did you force yourself to endure this?' His hand closed over her breast, his thumb rubbing lightly against her nipple, his lips continuing to drift across her face, teasing, tasting, his progress a leisurely one, his body hard against hers, as he moved slightly and pulled her against him, thigh pressed against thigh, his body infusing hers with slow heat, his lips continuing to brush against hers, his tongue stroking their soft outline.

'Ah, Sienna,' he breathed her name against her mouth, a soft caress. 'It won't work, you know. Outwardly you may seem cold, but inside . . .'

'Inside I'm cold too, Alexis,' she muttered through clenched teeth. 'I don't want you.'

'Keep on telling yourself that,' he taunted derisively, 'but it won't stop this.' He touched the pulse jumping frantically at the base of her throat, then slid his mouth moistly down to cover it, holding her imprisoned until she could feel the hard hammering of her blood in her veins. 'Or this . . .' his hand slid up under her tee shirt, his fingers light and determined against her breast, finding her peaking nipple unerringly, touching its hard betrayal, '. . . from telling me that you're a liar. And not just a liar, but a coward too. I never thought that of you before.'

'Words, Alexis,' she said tiredly, pulling away from him. 'I'm not carrying your child, by the way, and now I never will. I don't want you,

Alexis, and to impregnate me, you would have to force me.'

'*Would* I?' He moved swiftly, lifting her into his arms, striding towards the door that led to their bedroom. 'Would I, Sienna? I think not. You're far too hot-blooded for force to be needed. For all your innocence and inexperience you're the most sensual woman I've ever touched. I love watching your face when I make love to you, seeing the pleasure there, feeling your body's response to mine. Do you honestly expect me to believe that that was born of duty?'

He had reached their bedroom and pushed open the door, making his way unerringly to the bed in the darkness. 'Do you realise I cut short my business in Athens to come back to you?'

'Did you? She can't have been very pleased, but it was all for nothing, Alexis, you might as well go back.'

'She? Is that what you think?'

She shrugged, as he held her, searching her face in the fitful moonlight. 'Does it matter what I think? I'm not naïve enough to suppose I'm the only woman in your life, nor to misjudge the potency of your virility. After all, you've already proved to me that love has no place in your heart, that the sexual act is something that need not even be motivated by desire.'

'I presume you're talking about the first time we made love? Oh, you're wrong there, Sienna. I desired you. You'll never know how hard it was for me to do what I had to do then, to turn you away from my arms, but I had to think of Sofia. I'm not going to set you free. You can't remain cold in my arms for ever, I don't believe you could manage it even for one night ... I've missed having you in my bed, but you're not going to leave it again, Sienna. Before tonight's over, I'm going to hear you making those little sounds of pleasure deep in your throat, your body quivering with desire for me.'

'No!'

'Yes,' he said thickly, dropping her on the bed and coming down quickly alongside her, imprisoning her against the covers with the weight of his thighs.

She tried to resist him as his hands dealt with the barrier of her clothes, but he had the greater strength and, it seemed, the greater determination. His own shirt had come unbuttoned in the struggle, the scrape of his body hair against her soft skin faintly abrasive as she tried to wriggle free of the pressure of his weight against her, her fingers clawing angrily at his shoulders as she tensed her body against him.

'Scratch all you like,' Alexis muttered in her ear as he seized her wrists and pinned them together above her head with hard fingers, 'but before the night is over you will be offering me the salve of your kisses against the wounds you have just inflicted.'

'No!' Her eyes were hard and bright with anger, her body twisting as she tried to throw off his weight. He shifted slightly, still pinning her wrists, one hard, muscled thigh flung across hers, holding her against the bed, his eyes raking her flushed features and disordered curls before dropping slowly to rest on the pulse thudding visibly in her throat and then moving lower to where her breasts rose and fell with the urgency of her breathing. The rough pressure of his chest against their softness had hardened her nipples into thrusting points, spelling incitement rather than resistance, and Sienna felt humiliation clog her throat as Alexis studied the evidence of their arousal. He bent his head and she tensed, anticipating the arousing tug of his mouth against their hardness, but instead it was the soft curve of her waist he kissed, his mouth moving slowly across her skin. She forced herself to lie unmoving beneath his caress, to concentrate on the ache in her arms and not the warm, quivering sensations she could feel racing through her body where his mouth touched it. His free hand lay across her stomach, and she could feel the nerve endings jumping beneath it, the lazily spiralling circles he was drawing on her skin activating an inner spring that seemed to tighten in painful pleasure with each circumference of his flesh against her own. His mouth moved upwards, slowly, tasting her skin, his teeth nibbling it gently. It was a refined form of torture and she was sure that he knew it. Every instinct she possessed cried out for her to respond, to abandon her pride and lock her fingers in his hair, to hold his mouth against the aching burgeoning of her flesh, to move her hips beneath the heavy weight of his, her fingers running over his skin, her mouth tasting his warmth. But she must not; she must lie quiescent, uncaring, staring up at the ceiling, emptying her mind and body of everything but the fact that what she was fighting for wasn't a simple victory, but her very survival.

Alexis was still touching her, his lips slowly tracing a circle round her breast; he paused and Sienna opened her eyes. She was holding her breath and she forced herself to glance down over her own body towards him. Her face went white, her tongue touching dry lips. Even in the darkness there was enough light from the moon to show her the rounded outline of her breast, the darker flesh around her nipple pulsating in open hunger, as though straining towards the contact it wanted. 'You want me.' He said it flatly, his voice hard, but curiously empty. 'Say it, Sienna, say it!'

She shook her head, not able to trust her voice, and witnessed the dark fury that swept down over his face, his eyes glittering hotly between slitted lids as he moved and bent his head slowly towards her breast and then pausing to look into her eyes. Her heart was thudding like a sledgehammer. She tried to tug her wrists free, wanting to defend herself from the look in his eyes, but he refused to release her. His tongue touched the tender aureole of flesh, circled it slowly while she breathed in, her breath held against the agony of need Alexis was building inside her, too terrified to exhale in case she uttered the words he was wanting to hear, a mortal agony possessing her body as it fought against the control of her mind, wept and begged her to give way. Alexis hadn't moved. His tongue brushed over her nipple, an aching torment of pleasure, beneath which she wanted to moan and writhe with feverish urgency. His tongue was hot and moist against her. He had to stop. She couldn't endure much more. 'You want me.'

'No!'

'Liar.' He said it thickly, suddenly releasing her wrists and moving. The moment she felt the hard arousal of his body against her Sienna quivered. She knew that he had felt her instinctive response and bitterness tasted acid in her mouth. She raised her hands to his shoulders to push him away, mentally and physically exhausted by the strain of holding him at bay. She could not endure any more, but the touch of her fingers against his skin seemed to ignore something inside her. The self-control she had witnessed while he tormented her was gone, overwhelmed by a palpable surge of desire which gripped his body, perspiration breaking out on his skin, his hoarse, 'Damn you, Sienna!' hot against her ear, his arms tightening imprisoningly around her as his mouth closed over hers in a kiss that plunged her with him down into a dark spiralling cavern of need, which obliterated all her good resolutions and called out to that most primitive, secret part of her. Her hands slid from his shoulders to his nape, where they twined in his hair and then explored the ridged muscles of his throat, feeling them move against her touch, his skin moist, his hunger a physical force she couldn't withstand. He kissed her eyelids, and the soft spirals of her ears, her throat, and the vulnerable curve of her shoulders, his teeth biting into her skin, his kisses interspersed with muttered words she couldn't decipher.

'You may not want me, but I want you,' he told her hoarsely, returning to her lips, pulling sensuously at the lower one, running his tongue along its swollen fullness. 'No woman has driven me to this madness before. You arouse in me a hunger that nothing can appease.' He bent his head and found the hard crests of her breasts, running his tongue lightly from one to the other, letting her feel the tension invading his body, moving against her with a rhythmic urgency he seemed unable to control.

'Alexis, please stop this—please stop now. I can't stand any more!' The words were out before she could stop them. After all she had said to herself and to him she couldn't let him take her in anger, in punishment and nor could she give in to the demands of her own body, and touch and caress him as she was longing to do. She knew quite well what force drove him, how very potent was the desire that flared inside him, how hungry she was to share it, to be absorbed and possessed completely by it. She wanted to run her hands over the planes of his body, his broad chest, and narrow hips, the long leanness of his flanks, the firm masculine buttocks. She shuddered and pressed her hands to his chest. 'Alexis!'

'I can't. Sienna, I can't.' The thick, heated mutter broke through her anger and held her still beneath him. She heard him groan, a low hoarse sound of pain and need, and his body moved against hers, parting her thighs, his hands moving urgently downwards grazing against her breasts. His mouth touched one hard peak and Sienna held her breath, sensing that he was fighting for self-control, but as though the feel of her flesh fed a deep compulsive inner hunger, he tensed and then shuddered explosively, unable to prevent the driving thrust of his body against and inside her. She cried out, not in pain but in surprise that he should lose control, and his mouth took the cry, smothering it in heat, drawing her with him until she was part of the fierce, tumultuous pleasure he could no longer deny.

She woke up during the night, and knew by the tension in his body that he wasn't asleep. He seemed to know too that she was awake. She felt him turn over, his back towards her. 'I'll have the helicopter come over tomorrow,' he told her emotionlessly. 'You've won, Sienna. I'm setting you free.'

Free? Didn't he know that she would never be free?

'Am I allowed to know why?' Her voice was surprisingly dry.

'You mean you can't guess?' She sensed the derision behind his words. 'You drove me tonight to a pitch no woman has ever done before. I've always prided myself on my self-control, on my ability to reason, to weigh and judge. I can't trust myself where you're concerned any longer, Sienna—tonight proved that to me. I told myself I wouldn't take you until you asked me to. I wanted to prove to you that physically you *do* want me. Instead all I proved was that I was dangerously vulnerable. I didn't like the man you made me tonight, but I know now I can't make you any promises that there won't be another occasion when you will drive me to taking you as brutally as I once accused your brother of taking my sister. You bring out the worst in me, Sienna. You make me despise myself. If I keep you with me you'll probably destroy me, and because of that, because I *am* the man I am, in the interests of self-preservation I would have to find the means of destroying you first. I thought I could make it work between us, but I now know that I can't.'

She had found his Achilles heel, but it gave her no satisfaction. She had achieved what she had set out to achieve. Alexis would set her free. She knew it was better this way, that in the long run it would be less painful, but all she could think of was how much she had longed to kiss and caress him, how she had yearned to show her love, to melt in his arms and tell him that nothing else mattered. Now it was too late, and she promised herself that there were going to be no regrets. It was for the best, for both of them.

CHAPTER NINE

SIENNA left Athens three days later. Alexis insisted on accompanying her while she waited for her flight, just as he had insisted that she travel first class and accept the allowance he intended to give her, and which privately she had already decided to leave untouched. There was no pleasure in achieving her goal, her heart and body cried out to remain with Alexis, but what was the point? She wanted more, far more than he could ever give her, he had hurt and used her, but even knowing this there was no satisfaction to be found in the knowledge that she had forced him to change his mind and let her go. She hated the self-contempt in his eyes whenever he glanced towards her, and as she waited for her flight to be called, she wondered if he was remembering as she was doing the tortured, strained words he had muttered the night he had told her he was going to let her go.

'I can't keep you here now,' he had told her, 'not and keep my sanity and self-respect as well, because I can't promise myself that I won't be driven to taking you again, the way I took you tonight. You drive me beyond the limits of my self-control, Sienna. You were right—I should never have married you.'

She turned once as she went through the barrier. Alexis stood watching her, hands in the pockets of the dark, expensive suit he was wearing, the fabric stretched as tautly over his muscles as his flesh was stretched across the bones of his face. She knew he was suffering and stamped down hard on her longing to go to him and comfort him. His suffering sprang not from love but from bruised ego. He had thought himself completely in control, and the discovery that he wasn't lashed his pride in much the same way as her self-betrayal had lashed hers. Both of them were losers because of their coming together. They were better off apart—far better off.

The flight to London was uneventful. She took a taxi from the airport, telling herself that this would be her last extravagance before she stopped being a rich man's wife, and reverted to her former life style. Alexis had handed over to her before she left all the personal effects he had kept back from her while she was in hospital. Among them had been her key to Rob's flat, and she used it now, giving a surprised start when she heard footsteps on the other side of the door.

'Sienna!' Rob looked pale and tired, his hair rumpled as though he had been running irate fingers through it, a habit he had when annoyed. 'I've just got back and read your letter. What the devil's been going on?'

'If you let me get inside the door I'll tell you.' She had changed, Sienna acknowledged as she saw his brief frown. Before Rob had always been her adored and rather worshipped older brother, now he was someone she still loved but expected to meet on equal ground. 'What's all this about Stefanides? Is it true that you're married?'

'Yes. We're married, but it didn't work out.'

'You came to that decision pretty quickly, didn't you?' Rob's voice was dry, and Sienna knew she wasn't going to be allowed to get away with an abbreviated story. On the way home she had decided to tell Rob the truth. If she lied to him now she would have to go on lying, and she would make him see that the entire episode was over and that she wanted it forgotten, that revenge or retaliation were completely unnecessary.

She asked him to pour her a drink and saw his eyebrows lift again. She rarely drank, and never at home, but he poured her a measure of whisky and topped it up with water, handing the glass to her and then pouring another measure for himself.

'Right, I want to hear all about it, and I mean *all*, Sienna,' he told her curtly, 'Gill's told me that you met Stefanides at her office, and yet that night at the Savoy both of you behaved as though you'd never set eyes on one another before. Why?'

She could have told him that they had had a quarrel, she could have made up several small lies which would have covered the situation, but instead she told him the truth, starting at the beginning and telling the story with simple honesty, not trying to varnish any of the facts.

'No, Rob,' she said, shaking her head, and touching his arm restrainingly, when she had described what happened at the cottage, and she could see the anger burning up inside him. 'The blame wasn't Alexis' alone. I wanted him to make love to me. I should have been mature enough to see that a man like him wouldn't fall instantly in love with an immature fool like me. Perhaps deep down inside I did suspect it, but I wouldn't allow myself to listen to my suspicions. Of course, when he found out the truth, he was stunned.'

'I'm sure he was,' Rob agreed tightly. 'God, the bastard! When I think . . .'

'Well, don't. It's over, Rob, and it would have been over even sooner if Alexis hadn't decided to play knight errant and marry me after my accident.'

'Yes,' Rob frowned, 'that's something I can't understand. Why should he marry you?'

'He wanted to make amends, or at least that's what he said to me. He felt his "honour" demanded it. And then there was the possibility that I might be carrying his child.'

'But why marry you? He could simply have bought you off—that's the way rich men's minds normally work. And to make love to you in the first place. . . . He must have wanted you, Sienna.'

'Must he?'

'Yes, I think so.' Rob glanced at her speculatively. 'And you—how do you feel now?'

'I . . .'

'The truth. Let's have the truth between us at least.'

'I love him,' Sienna admitted simply, 'but I couldn't live with him as his wife, having his children, knowing that all he felt for me was a combination of guilt and physical desire—the same physical desire he could presumably have felt for any halfway attractive female who crossed his path.'

'There's something here that doesn't add up,' muttered Rob. 'I can't work out what it is, but it just doesn't make sense. What do you plan to do now that you're back?'

'Alexis wanted to make me an allowance,' she pulled a wry face. 'I can't take it, but I didn't tell him that. I thought I might go back to the cottage. Dad's publishers want to reissue his books, but they need bringing up to date—I think I could do that. It was something he was working on before he died. I have most of his notes.'

'Running away?'

She grimaced again. 'Let's just say I need a

breathing space and somewhere to hide while I lick my wounds.'

'I wonder why he let you go, after being so insistent about marrying you in the first place?' Rob had a reporter's mind and would worry at the loose ends like a dog with a bone, Sienna suspected. The one thing she hadn't told her brother was that final scene with Alexis. Her resistance, her refusal to admit that his touch did arouse her, that she did want him, had been the fuel which ignited his anger, and she was no more proud of forcing him to lose control than he was of having done so. She knew without the need for him to put it into words that he had taken her in rage and frustration, wanting to break her resistance, wanting almost to destroy her in the heat of his fury, and she could well understand why a man like Alexis would find that knowledge an unbearable burden.

'Mmm . . . well, if that's what you want to do. I have some news for you as well.'

Sienna eyed her brother. 'Has it anything to do with Gill?'

He stared at her suspiciously, 'And if it has?'

'Oh, nothing,' Sienna told him smugly. 'It's just that it's high time the two of you stopped pretending. You do love her, don't you, Rob?'

'Yes, but I also love my job, and that was the problem. Gill made it clear to me that she wanted a husband whom she could count on to be there. I couldn't make the sort of promises she wanted, but the problem seems to have resolved itself, at least for the time being. I've been commissioned to do a book comparing the world's trouble-spots, to try and find reasons, explanations—you know the sort of thing. This trip was my last one. By the time the book is finished, no doubt I'll be too old to go out in the field.'

'And you're willing to give it up?' She was surprised, because she knew how much Rob loved his job.

'Let's just say I'm more willing to give up the job than I am Gill. I had a near miss this last time, and as I lay there listening to bullets whining all around me, all I could think of was Gill. I decided there and then that life's too short to waste in quarrelling.'

'Well, I'm pleased for you both. When's the wedding to be?'

'As soon as we can arrange it. I was going to write to you to tell you all this. In fact, I'd have been on my way out to Micros right now if it hadn't been for Gill. I couldn't believe that you'd actually married Stefanides, and then Gill told me about how the two of you first met.' Rob looked at his sister oddly. 'She seemed to think it was love at first sight, for both of you. She told me that you looked stunned and she could well understand why, but that Stefanides looked as though someone had just poleaxed him.'

'Probably the relief at having found me,' Sienna said flippantly. 'Heavens, I'm tired! I think I'll go to bed now, Rob. I'll leave for home in the morning, so you needn't worry that I'll be hanging around to cramp your style,' she teased, ducking to avoid the cushion he flung at her.

She was just finishing her packing when she heard the doorbell. Her first initial instinctive hope that it might be Alexis was stifled as she saw Gill's outline through the glass.

'Sienna! Rob's told me everything. Oh, my poor

dear, and I thought the two of you were so well matched!'

'These things happen. Tell me about your plans for the wedding,' Sienna demanded, changing the subject. 'How far have you got with them?'

Gill allowed herself to be distracted and dutifully told Sienna about the fuss her mother was making, expressing her own surprise. 'I honestly thought Ma wouldn't mind where the ceremony took place as long as it was legal, but oh no, she wants the full bit, village wedding, reception on the lawn, church, choirboys, all the cousins as bridesmaids. . . .'

'And?'

Gill grimaced slightly. 'And Rob's siding with her—says we might as well have the photographs to show our grandchildren! But you and Alexis—is there any chance that. . . .?'

Sienna shook her head. 'No.'

'But the two of you seemed so much in love.'

'You were the one who warned me against him, remember?' Sienna said sardonically.

'Yes, I know, but that was only when I thought his intentions were strictly dishonourable. I never doubted how he felt about you, it was so obvious. I'd read about "naked desire", but the way he looked at you when he walked into my office, I was almost on the verge of feeling jealous!'

Sienna was sure that Gill was exaggerating, but she said nothing, and having extracted a promise from her to help out as much as she could with the wedding, Gill left.

An hour later Sienna herself was on her way to the Cotswolds. Mrs Mallors came across when she saw her car, and asked anxiously how she was feeling. 'Terrible how your accident happened. It was fortunate that your young man was there to take charge. I cleaned up the cottage and locked it up as he asked, and I've been in a few times to dust round and keep an eye on things. You've got a good colour. Been away, have you?'

'In Greece,' Sienna told her, glad that she had had the foresight to remove Alexis' rings from her finger, and at the same time cursing her sentimentality in putting them on the fine gold chain she wore round her neck. She could feel the weight of the gold and precious stones between her breasts. She should have sent them back to Alexis, what was the point in hanging on to them? All they would do was serve as a reminder of the past, of the agony of loving and leaving him.

She spent the next few days going through her father's papers, sorting out his notes, and generally preparing for the task of revising his books. Most of the work had been done prior to his death, but the task was still a challenging one. She went to Cheltenham to meet her father's publisher to discuss how best to approach the work. They had lunch together, and afterwards she strolled through the town, admiring the Regency façades and the curving terraces. Like all famous spa towns, it had an elegance that refused to fade, and she wondered with irony how many people would be admiring twentieth-century architecture in two centuries to come!

When she got back she started work, gradually finding herself becoming more and more involved in what she was doing. Time seemed to slip away, and although she knew she was using her work as an anaesthetic, working was the only way she could blot out the pain. It demanded the whole of her concentration, and if she worked long enough it was possible for her to drop into bed and fall asleep without being tormented by her memories.

She had been in the cottage just over a week when she caught a glimpse of herself in the mirror one morning and frowned over what she saw. Her skin was pale, her eyes huge and dark in her triangular face.

'What you need, my girl, is some fresh air,' she told herself. The work was coming along quite nicely and there was no reason why she should not take some time off. The garden cried out for attention, but pulling up weeds would give her too much time to think, she needed something more demanding.

In the end she settled for what had once been a favourite walk. It involved a long haul up a steepish hill, but the benefits once the top was gained were worthwhile. She sat in the lee of the hillside gazing at the panorama spread below her, her skin caressed by the July sun.

The wind changed, blowing up clouds, and she decided regretfully that it was time to leave. She had just gained the top of the village street when she saw the car. It was parked outside the cottage, black and slightly sinister—an expensive car, and not one she recognised, and her heartbeat quickened in time to her footsteps, a soft flush warming her skin. Alexis! Had he come to find her, to . . .? She hesitated outside the front door, shivering a little as she tried to come to terms with her feelings. Would she have the strength to turn him away? She pushed open the door and walked into the sitting room, her face giving her away as she saw her visitor. 'Sofia!' she exclaimed.

Sofia was sitting down, reading a magazine, but she got up quickly when she saw Sienna. 'Please forgive my intrusion, but your neighbour let me in. She said you would not mind.'

'No, of course not. Would you like a cup of tea, coffee. . . .?'

'Coffee would be lovely.'

'I hope you haven't been waiting long,' Sienna called from the kitchen. 'I've been out for a walk.'

'I arrived just after lunch. I had some difficulty discovering where you were, but your sister-in-law prevailed upon your brother to give me your address.'

That meant she couldn't have come from Alexis. He would have known this address and would have told her how to find it. 'You'll have to excuse Rob, he's feeling rather over-protective at the moment.'

'Yes, I can understand that. What Alexis did was a terrible thing, but he is my brother and I too feel a need to . . . protect him. . . .'

Sienna stiffened slightly, putting down the tray of coffee. 'Alexis needs no protection from me,' she assured her. 'Had I been conscious and in full possession of my memory I would never have married him. He knew that, Sofia.'

'Yes, I know. I have talked to him and he has told me it all. He is very ashamed, Sienna . . . very disturbed. He is a very proud man, and the knowledge. . . .'

'Please, I don't want to talk about it. I do understand how Alexis feels, but guilt and a need to make reparation, these are not good bases for marriage.'

'He is not well, Sienna,' Sofia told her. 'He is under a tremendous amount of strain. I have never seen him like this, not even when my parents were drowned. He has decided to sell off most of his companies, and he is thinking about living fulltime on Micros. I am afraid for him, can you believe that? Always he has been the stronger, the person I could turn to and rely on. Constantin tells me I should not worry. He is a marvellous husband and I love him dearly, but he does not know Alexis as I do. He needs you, Sienna. He misses you dreadfully, and I am sure it is only his pride that prevents him from asking you to go back. You love him.' It was a statement of fact, and Sienna inclined her head in acknowledgement. 'Surely then that is the basis you are looking for.'

'Perhaps for some women, but I'm sure that you would not want to be married to a man who merely tolerates you, who endures you because he feels he must.'

Sofia paled, and Sienna knew her words had hit home. 'On the night he first became my lover Alexis told me that he didn't love me. He told me why he'd made love to me.'

'And that is something you cannot forget or forgive,' Sofia said softly. 'Could it not be that he said those words to you to reinforce his purpose to himself as much as to you? Could he not have been punishing himself for ... for caring about you? I know my brother, Sienna. Despite what is printed in the gossip columns he has never indulged in meaningless affairs.'

'Of course not,' Sienna agreed lightly, 'and ours was not meaningless either. On the contrary, he told me how much satisfaction it gave him to know that you were avenged. Making love to me was extremely meaningful, but that meaning had nothing to do with love. If Alexis really wanted me, Sofia, do you suppose he wouldn't find some way of telling me so?'

'After you have rejected him?' Sofia shook her head sadly. 'You do not know my brother well if you think that. Perhaps I should explain to you how it was for him as a child. I only know because my mother told me. She was his second cousin, and only twelve years older than him. His father showed him no affection. He didn't want to spoil him, he wanted him to grow up tough and strong. I remember my mother telling me that as a child Alexis had a dog whom he adored, and that this animal was knocked down and killed by a car. Alexis wept as though his heart would break—he was only seven at the time, but when his father saw him he told him to stop. No son of mine ever cries, he said to him, and Alexis was sent to his room until he had learned to behave like a true Stefanides.

'Alexis loved our father, but there was never affection between them. I never once saw my father reach out and embrace him in the way that Greek fathers do their children. He rejected Alexis, Sienna, just as you have rejected him.'

Sofia left shortly afterwards and Sienna watched her go in sadness. In other circumstances they could have been friends, but she could not explain to his sister exactly why Alexis would not want her back.

CHAPTER TEN

'THE wedding's fixed for August, and I thought it might be a good idea if you could come up to London this week and we can chat about the arrangements. I can never remember all I want to say on the phone. Can you come?'

'I don't see why not.' Gill had rung up just as Sienna finished her breakfast and she glanced at the small calendar on the wall as she spoke. 'Any day will suit me.'

'How about tomorrow, then, I'm pretty clear then. Stay overnight and we'll all go out.'

After she had hung up Sienna stared out of the kitchen window. It was three days since she had received her visit from Sofia, and there hadn't been a single hour in any of them when she hadn't thought about Alexis. Seeing Sofia had reactivated all the old wounds. She lay in bed at night, aching to feel him beside her. There had been no correspondence between them, and Sienna wondered when he intended to start proceedings for divorce. They had agreed on Micros that the sooner it was all over the better. Perhaps she ought to try and see a solicitor when she was in London. It seemed ironic that she should be planning her divorce while her brother was planning his wedding.

She reached London shortly after ten in the morning and went directly to Gill's office. Gill beamed when she saw her and offered her a cup of coffee. 'Ten minutes and then I'll be ready. I want you to come with me and help me buy my dress.

I've earmarked a couple, but I can't make the final decision. We've decided to go for the whole bit,' she added pulling a face, 'and Ma's over the moon! You've lost weight.' She eyed Sienna and frowned, but fortunately the phone rang before she could make any comment.

They spent the rest of the morning shopping. Sienna opted for her second choice of dress. Full-length and made of pale apricot chiffon, it suited Gill's olive skin colouring and dark hair.

'I thought a hat to go with it,' Gill said uncertainly. 'What do you think?'

They found one by Frederick Fox in a toning apricot, and Sienna allowed herself to be persuaded into one in pale cream to go with the suit she had decided to wear.

'How about lunch?' Gill asked when they stepped out of the shop. 'I'm whacked!'

Over lunch they talked about the wedding, or rather Gill talked and Sienna listened. Rob and Gill were keeping on Rob's flat where they would live when they were married. 'I'm keeping on the agency, for the time being anyway, but Rob's anxious to start a family, and he's even talking about looking for a house in the Cotswolds.'

After lunch they shopped for underwear and shoes. Gill was indefatigable, and Sienna felt exhausted when she finally called a halt. 'I think I'll have to forgo tonight,' she said when they reached the flat. 'I'm tired out, and besides, I don't want to play gooseberry.' Gill laughed but didn't demur. 'Rob said to tell you he won't be back until about eight. He's booked the table for nine, so see how you feel then. Thanks for your help, by the way. Tomorrow I start on furniture.' She saw Sienna's expression and laughed. 'Yes, that's exactly how Rob looked when I told him, but this place needs a thorough overhaul, it's mostly junk shop stuff, and Rob says I can have a free hand. My godfather has come up trumps with a very generous cheque as well.'

It was just gone five when Gill left. Sienna made herself a mug of coffee and switched on the television, settling down to watch the news. The main items came first, and she lay back in her chair trying to relax. The day had been a trying one, not just because it was so tiring, but she hadn't been able to stop thinking about her own wedding, comparing it to Gill's. 'Alexis Stefanides,' she heard the newsreader say, the words cutting across her thoughts and jerking her to full attention, 'often referred to by the press as "the Greek tycoon" is presently in London presiding over the disposal of some of his company assets.' The picture cut to a busy street scene, and Sienna held her breath as she saw Alexis' familiar features. Her first thought was that Sofia was right. He had lost weight, and his face looked saturnine and faintly sallow. He was stepping out of a car, and the reporter hurried forward, asking for his comments. 'My only comment is that there comes a time in every man's life when he realises that he is spending far too much time in the boardroom. I have now reached that time.'

'And do you intend to dispose of all your companies, Mr Stefanides?'

'No, some I shall retain, those which are easiest to control' The interview was at an end, Alexis walked forward into the foyer of the Savoy and the picture cut back to the main news reader.

Alexis was in London, and now she knew the reason for his loss of weight and changed appearance. No doubt it was because of all the business deals he was involved in. Sofia was deluding herself when she believed it was on her account. She switched off the television and roamed edgily round the room. Alexis here in London! She gnawed at her bottom lip. She had heard nothing from him about their divorce; perhaps she ought to go and see him? Would he see her? She could think of no reason why he should not. After all, he was not affected by her presence the way she was by his. He had nothing to betray or conceal.

Making up her mind, she hurried to her room, gathering up a change of clothes. She still felt hot and sticky from their shopping expedition, and if she had learned one thing from life, it was that feeling confident about one's appearance always helped one to appear confident.

She showered and dressed quickly in a soft lemon suit she had bought before her accident. The waist was slightly loose, and she pulled a face as she notched the belt tighter, and slipped into toning yellow shoes. She rang for a taxi, and brushed her hair while she waited, not allowing herself to have second thoughts. The taxi arrived promptly, and she stepped into it, giving the driver her destination.

When they reached the Savoy and she got out the butterflies which had been making tentative forays in her stomach swarmed in full strength. Almost she turned round and went back, but then she reminded herself that it was better to get everything sorted out, better to end their marriage as quickly and painlessly as they could.

When she asked for Alexis' room number she was slightly surprised by the startled look she received from the receptionist. 'Mr Stefanides?' she repeated, but she didn't ask Sienna if Alexis was expecting her, which surprised her a little. She simply called over one of the staff, and murmured something to him.

'If you would come this way.' The lift bore Sienna upwards and stopped at the familiar floor, the porter leading the way to Alexis' suite. He stopped outside, inserting the key in the lock, and pushed open the door for her. Thanking him, Sienna stepped inside. Perhaps Alexis was expecting someone and they had had instructions to show them up? That meant that he wasn't in the hotel at present, Sienna decided, her heart sinking a little. She hadn't anticipated that, which was surely a little foolish of her, but in her anxiety to see him and get everything sorted out she hadn't stopped to think of the difficulties. Well, she was here now, and sooner or later Alexis was bound to return. All she had to do was wait.

She sat down in one of the chairs, glancing round the familiar sitting room. The typewriter she had used was still there, and she wondered who was using it now. She got up and prowled round nervously, touching the wooden surfaces of the tables, trying to calm her overwrought nerves. A small sound from the bedroom stopped her, and she paused, listening, icy tremors of apprehension sliding down her spine. Who was in the bedroom? She heard another sound, and although it was distorted by the closed door, it sounded like a groan. A variety of feverish images raced through her mind. Alexis had been attacked and was lying hurt beyond the door . . . someone had broken in . . . someone had. . . .

Resolutely she pushed open the door, coming to

a full stop at what she saw, Alexis *was* in the suite after all. He was lying in the large double bed, his unshaven beard darkening his jaw with stubble, his eyes closed, a hectic flush of fever burning his skin, completely oblivious to her presence. Sienna walked over to the bed and stared down at him, chewing her bottom lip. She reached out and touched his skin. It scorched her fingertips, a burning dry heat, which sent warning messages flashing to her brain. This was no ordinary sleep, but what was Alexis doing here, lying here ill? He was a millionaire, and yet in that moment it struck her how alone he was that he could lie ill in a hotel bedroom with no one of his own beside him. She dropped to her knees beside the bed, stroking the dark hair back off his forehead, her anguished, 'Oh, Alexis!' not even penetrating his fevered sleep. She couldn't leave him like this. He needed a doctor, and at once. She went back into the sitting room and picked up the phone. 'This is Mrs Stefanides,' she said crisply to the girl at the other end. 'My husband is ill and needs a doctor.'

There was a moment's silence and then the girl said in confusion, 'But, Mrs Stefanides, the doctor has already arrived. One of our porters showed her up to the suite, ten minutes ago. . . .' she broke off, then said, 'Oh, please excuse me, there has been some mistake—the doctor is here now. I can't understand what has happened.'

'It's quite all right,' Sienna soothed her. So that was why they had let her into the suite—they had mistaken her for the doctor! She smiled to herself. Did she look like a doctor? She wouldn't have thought so.

Five minutes later when she heard the knock on the outer door she flew to open it. 'So your husband is ill again, Mrs Stefanides? Well, I warned him last night that he was overdoing things. He has had a very severe fever.' The doctor glanced curiously at Sienna. 'I didn't realise he was married, but now that I do it explains a good deal. Your name wouldn't be Sienna, by any chance, would it?' He was a Scot and his voice broadened faintly over her name, his burr more noticeable.

'Yes, it would.'

'Ah, then you are the young lady he has been calling for. I wondered. . . . A quarrel, I suppose. They happen in the best of families, although your timing was a little bit off. I suppose he's been a bit tetchy, hard to live with—is that it? I told him last night he should never have travelled.'

'What exactly is the matter with ... with my husband?' Sienna asked huskily, watching him examine the sleeping form.

'A touch of malaria. He picked it up in his teens, apparently, somewhere in South America, and these things can flare up from time to time. I suspect your husband has been under a considerable emotional and mental strain. That often contributes towards weakening one's resistance, which is why he's suffering a particularly nasty attack this time, and he wouldn't heed my advice that he ought to rest. Perhaps he'll listen to you. I'll give him an injection now, and if he's no better in the morning, call me and I'll come back. Otherwise I'll look in on him again tomorrow afternoon. If you take my advice you won't let him leave that bed for at least three days, and then when he does he needs a long restful holiday.'

'I'll do my best,' Sienna told him shakily, knowing that she didn't have the right to make any plans for Alexis' future.

'You'll stay with him mind?' the doctor asked her. 'He shouldn't really be left alone. He needs to be kept warm, but when the fever breaks and he starts to sweat he might get a little violent, throw off the bedclothes, that sort of thing.'

'Yes, of course I will.'

Sienna waited until the doctor had gone to ring Rob and explain the position. Strangely enough he did not demur when she told him what she planned to do. 'We'll expect you when we see you, then,' was his only comment.

When she put the receiver down Sienna went back into the bedroom. Alexis had turned over and was lying on his chest, his face buried in the pillows, his back exposed. She went across and drew the covers over him, and he muttered something thickly. His skin still burned where she touched it, and on some impulse she couldn't quell she bent her head and lightly kissed his bare shoulder. He shuddered beneath her touch, and to her dismay she heard him groan her name. His eyelashes fluttered and for a moment she thought he was going to wake, but the drug the doctor had given him was too powerful and his body subsided, relaxing beneath her stroking touch. When she was sure he was asleep Sienna pulled the covers over his back and closed the door.

Alone in the sitting room, she found the large diary she knew he kept and went through it systematically, cancelling his appointments to give him the three days resting period the doctor had suggested. Only when she was satisfied that she had done everything she could to ensure that no problems would arise did Sienna call room service and ask for a light snack to be sent up.

'If he should rouse, don't worry about it,' the

doctor had told her before he left. 'He'll be rather vague and probably not make much sense, if he does come round. Sleep is what he needs right now, the body's best recuperative weapon.'

She kept the door between the sitting room and Alexis' bedroom open while she ate, the lamps dimmed low so that the light would not disturb him. He seemed less restless, and she picked up a book, trying to concentrate on it, hoping that the doctor was right when he said that Alexis should sleep.

It was just after midnight when he stirred, his eyes opening and focusing directly on her with a brilliance that surprised her.

'Sienna?'

She got up and walked across to the bed. 'Yes, it's me. I hope you don't mind.'

'Mind?' He laughed bitterly. 'God, it only needed that! Are you real, I wonder? I have imagined you here so often these last few days that. . . .'

'I'm real, Alexis.' She reached out and touched him lightly. 'No, don't get up,' she told him when he started to move. 'The doctor says you've got to stay in bed. He came earlier and gave you a shot. . . .'

'And summoned you to nurse me?' he grimaced faintly.

'I'm sorry if you don't want me here. I saw you on television and wanted to see you. . . .'

'Wanted to see me?' He laughed harshly. 'Oh no, Sienna, you didn't *want*, you've never wanted—you proved that beyond all shadow of any doubt on Micros, didn't you?' He spoke so savagely, so bitterly that for a moment she was silent. She had known she had angered him, but had never dreamed he would feel this bitterness, this ferocity she could see burning deep in his eyes, this sickness that seemed to eat into him when he looked at her.

'Alexis, you're sick,' she said quietly. 'You. . . .'

'Oh, yes, I'm sick all right,' he agreed. He struggled to sit up and dislodged the sheet, his body gleaming beneath the faint light. 'What is it the Bible says? Feed me on green apples, for I am sick of love. Does it amuse you to know what causes my sickness, Sienna? Is that why you are here to gloat over me? To torment me with all that I cannot have?'

'Alexis, you don't know what you're saying.' She must remember that the doctor had warned her that he might ramble. He certainly seemed to be doing so now.

'Don't I?' His eyes glittered strangely, hectic colour staining his skin. 'Or is it that you simply don't *want* to hear? That would be the perfect punishment, wouldn't it, Sienna? I refused the gift of your love when you would have given it willingly, and now I am reduced to a beggar at the gates, forbidden to even dream!'

'Alexis, you don't love me.'

'How tender-hearted you are, even when you reject me!' he jeered. He moved, dislodging more of the covers, and Sienna leaned over automatically to pull them up, careful of the doctor's advice. Her fingers grazed accidentally across the smooth hot flesh of his stomach and he tensed, hard fingers curling round her wrist, forcibly pushing her away. When she looked up he was trembling, perspiration sheening on his skin. 'For God's sake don't touch me,' he muttered hoarsely. 'You don't want to believe I love you because you don't want to hurt me. I know you, Sienna, you don't like to cause others pain. I thought I could hold you, feed your hunger for me until you forgot that you had stopped loving me.'

'But, Alexis. . . .'

'No.' He dropped back against the pillows, his eyes closed, exhaustion drawing deep grooves either side of his mouth. 'No, don't say anything. I set out to use you, but in the end my vengeance rebounded on me. I told myself it was desire that fuelled my hunger, physical desire of you and mental desire for the revenge I had sworn my sister would have. That night in the cottage. . . .'

'The night you told me the truth,' Sienna said tonelessly.

'What truth?' His eyes opened and what she saw in their depths made her gasp. 'What I told you was the lies I was telling myself, the lies I *had* to tell myself if I wanted to retain my sanity. I loved you, but I could not allow myself to love you. You were a disposable pawn, I had already committed myself to the path I must take, I had sworn on my father's grave that Sofia would be revenged. And then I discovered the truth.' He grimaced and shuddered deeply. 'That was when the full macabre humour of the Greek myths came home to me. Remember Theseus?' he asked her. She nodded, wondering if he really knew what he was saying. His mind might wander, the doctor had told her.

'Thesèus was sent with the children of tribute to Crete, and before he left he promised his father he would return within a year alive and well. His father the King of Athens asked that if he did manage to escape from Crete, he change the sail of his boat, so that he would know he was safe. On

Crete Theseus and his fellow prisoners managed to escape from the labyrinth, which was the home of the dreaded Minotaur, the monster that was half man and half bull, with the aid of the King's daughter, Ariadne, but in his joy at escaping, Theseus forgot to change the sail, and when his father saw the boat approaching Athens, he believed his son to be dead and killed himself. The moral of that story is that even in our moments of greatest achievement, or greatest success, Nemesis lurks, waiting to remind us that we are only human and very vulnerable—dangerously vulnerable in my case.'

Sienna leaned towards him, tears shimmering in her eyes, wanting to ease the pain she could see he was feeling, but he tensed and shrank back. 'No, don't touch me. Can't you see,' he groaned despairingly, 'I only have to touch you and I forget everything but my need for you. Do you want to destroy me completely, Sienna? Is that to be *your* revenge? I can't live with the memory of what I did to you, do you know that? I can't sleep for remembering how it was when you couldn't remember, when you accepted me as your husband . . . your lover.' He closed his eyes and shivered, the fever breaking.

Could she believe him? Sienna glanced down at the bed, a warm tide of feeling sweeping through her, destroying the barriers of pride and pain. She reached out and touched his stubbly jaw, wondering at the vulnerability of him. When he was better would he remember what he had said to her, or would he always carry around inside him the barbs she had planted, festering and growing. Could she wipe out what she had done? 'I thought you wanted me,' he had said, and she had, but she had withheld the truth from him and let him destroy himself in trying to force it from her. Even if he did love her, even if she admitted that she loved him, could there be a future for them together with those barbs still festering?

'Sienna?' He opened his eyes and muttered her name thickly.

'I'm here.'

'Tell me that you believe me. I love you,' he whispered fiercely, 'I love you.'

'I love you too.'

He shook his head. 'No—you feel sorry for me. Do you think I don't know the difference?' He smiled sardonically. 'If you loved me why did you leave me? No, Sienna, thank you for your pity, but it is not what I want. What you said was quite true. You responded to me when you thought you ought to, because your mind kept the truth from you, but once the truth was revealed, my touch chilled you, you turned to ice in my arms, and I, God help me, didn't even have the grace to release you. My crime was a thousand times worse than that of which I accused your brother. I raped you,' he said bleakly, and she saw the suffering in his eyes. 'I loved you, and I hurt you.'

'No.' She shook her head, and reached for his hand. 'I wanted you, Alexis, you were quite right about that.' He was watching her, his eyes burning into hers, but she could see he didn't believe her. 'I want you now,' she whispered the words shakily, but there was still no response. How could she make him believe her? How could she show him that. . . . She tensed and glanced at him, moistening her dry lips with the tip of her tongue. 'Shall I show you how much?' He didn't move, but she could see the sudden tensing of his muscles, the dark flare of hunger in his eyes that nothing could conceal. As she pushed aside the bedclothes she sent up a silent prayer that her guardian angel, if she had one, was watching over her now. What she was going to do took all her courage, all her love, and so much more besides, and if she failed. . . .

She set her teeth and quickly removed her own clothes, all the time watching Alexis. He made no move to touch her, and she wished she had turned off the lamp in the sitting room, and that her task might have been accomplished with the benefit of concealing darkness.

When she had finished she faced him proudly. There was no response, unless she counted the sudden ridging of muscles in this throat and the darkly possessive gleam betrayed in his eyes before he closed them.

So much depended on her getting it right, on her rebuilding what she had destroyed. She pushed back the covers until his body was completely exposed, her breath fluttering in her throat. She had told him she loved him, she had told him she wanted him, she would now show him the depths of her capacity to feel both. She had never even dreamed of doing anything like this before, and the balance must be finely weighed.

She stroked her fingers lightly over his taut shoulders, then bent her head to follow their touch with the warm pressure of her lips. Against his throat she whispered how much she wanted him, letting her body make its own admissions, feeling the pulse thud and race beneath his skin where her mouth touched, but still Alexis made no sign of acceptance, of understanding or responding to her words. She moved downwards, telling herself that she had known it would not be easy, that he had been badly savaged by their final encounter, pouring out her love, letting her senses dictate her actions, lingering in her worship of his body, touching it with reverence and joy, wanting to show him her need to touch him rather than a mere desire to arouse him. His stomach quivered under her caress, and he made a small sound that might have been a protest. His hands lay flat against the bed, palms down, but the knuckles gleamed painfully through his skin, and seeing that bolstered her wavering courage.

'Alexis, I want you so badly—please love me!' Each whispered admission eased something of her own pain, each touch of her hands and mouth against his body reinforcing them. She stroked his thighs, feeling the abrasiveness of the dark hair shadowing them, against her tongue, hearing his sharply indrawn breath and glorying cautiously in it. Her lips brushed his toes, her palms stroking over his calves. Surely by now he must know she was speaking the truth?

She raised her head and looked up at him. His eyes were closed, his face the colour of parchment. She worked her way back up over his body, trying to show him with every caress the quality of her love. By the time she reached his throat again every muscle in his hard frame was locked, and she ached with tension and in sympathy with the agony of mind she knew he was enduring. She touched his throat tentatively with her lips and knew that her self-imposed control was starting to crack. She couldn't go on much longer. If he didn't respond soon. 'Alexis, please, please love me. . . .' she had no need to think of what she should say now, the words tumbled out feverishly, matching the hot little kisses she was scattering over his face.

Her tongue touched his lips and she was trembling so badly she couldn't stop. Tears formed and welled from her eyes, desperation sharpening her senses, her body soft and fluid as she pressed it against his, whispering pleas for his love against his skin.

'Alexis, I love you so much!'

He moved, his arms locking round her, rolling her beneath him, his voice thick as he muttered, 'You'd better mean that, Sienna, because God help me, I'm going to love you anyway, and if you're lying you're going to destroy us both.'

His mouth burned against her skin, touching her as she had longed for him to touch her all the time they had been apart. He found the impatient peaks of her breasts and eased the aching pain from them with the warmth of his mouth, his hands sliding down over her body showing her the arousal he had fought to control when she touched him.

She cried out as he entered her, lost in the pleasure of being with him, murmuring her love with incoherent, panted cries until his mouth silenced her, echoing the hunger of his body.

Fierce, primitive pleasure swept through her, her body delighting in the capitulation of his, responding to and encouraging his avid response. He cried out her name as the moment of climax seized them both, and the way he said it was balm to her aching heart. She was dimly conscious of him telling her he loved her as she slid down from the heights, and of trying to respond, but exhaustion was sweeping through her, and all she wanted was to sink against his body, to be cushioned and protected by it.

'Good morning. *You* slept well!' Sienna turned her

head, her eyes opening to their widest extent as she saw Alexis grinning back at her. For a moment she felt totally confused, and then it all came rushing back. Stupidly she flushed, not a soft pink, but a deep dark red, and as though he knew the reason for her embarrassment Alexis laughed softly, and bent his head towards her, nibbling the soft curves of her throat. 'Still love me?'

Her lashes shielded her eyes from him. 'Yes.'

'Still want me?' His hand slid beneath the sheet and found the outline of her breast. 'Are you going to show me?'

She looked up at him, but there was no mockery in his eyes, only a wicked dancing amusement, the satisfaction of a man who is well pleased by the effect of his masculinity on the woman in his life. Sienna felt her spirits lift and said demurely, 'Are you going to show *me*? After all it must be your turn.'

Her answer seemed to satisfy him, because he pulled her against him and murmured into her throat. 'So, no excuses ... no denials that it happened, no more telling me that you don't want or love me?'

'After all the trouble I went to prove that I *did*?'

His eyes danced. 'Mmm ... I think perhaps I gave in too easily. Are you sure you don't want to convince me all over again?' His thumb stroked her nipple and her body flared into urgent life, arching unashamedly against him, her mouth parting beneath his, her soft sigh of pleasure bringing an answering groan from his throat.

'You're supposed to be recuperating,' Sienna reminded him when he at last released her.

'So I am—like I told you, losing you was what made me ill.'

'The doctor diagnosed it as malaria.'

'So it was,' Alexis agreed promptly, 'but very much exacerbated by my mental and emotional vulnerability. Sienna. . . .' He held her face between his hands, suddenly serious. 'Why did you do it?'

She didn't need to ask what he meant.

'Because it was the only way I could protect myself. I love you so much, Alexis. I couldn't stay with you as your wife, believing you didn't love me. I had to get you to send me away.'

'Yes.' In that one word of acceptance of everything. 'When you ran out of the cottage and I heard that car. . . .' He shuddered. 'I shouldn't have married you the way I did, but I knew then I could never let you go. I knew once you were well you'd never agree to see me again. At that time we didn't know about your memory. I took a chance, telling myself I could make it work, that my love was enough for both of us, that you must still have some feeling for me. I knew I'd hurt you—and badly,' his mouth compressed, 'but I told myself I'd make it all right. When I found out you'd lost your memory I took the coward's way out. I thought once we were lovers . . . once you had accepted me as your husband.'

'We've both made mistakes, both been less than honest with one another.'

'And now. . . .'

'The doctor said you needed to rest—at least three days in bed was his prescription,' Sienna said mischievously, 'and then a good long holiday.'

'Mmm . . . was that as well as the three days in bed, or because of it, do you suppose?' Alexis asked dryly. 'Sienna, about last night. . . .' She looked down at his chest, curling her toes into the mattress. 'I told myself I wouldn't accept your pity, that there was no way you could convince me that you cared for me. My pride took a bad beating that last time, and. . . .'

'And?' Sienna prompted softly.

'Oh, God, you little witch, you know exactly what I mean!' Alexis groaned, tilting her chin so that he could look at her. 'If I didn't know for sure that there'd been no other men, right now I'd be asking myself just where you learned to. . . .'

'To?' she prompted.

'To pour out your love, in a libation. To give so generously of yourself."

'I didn't think our love stood any chance unless I could convince you completely that I'd lied when I said I didn't want you, and I couldn't think of any other way,' she told him. 'I didn't just want to show that I wanted you, I wanted you to know how completely I. . . .'

His fingers brushed her lips. 'I do know, but let me hear you say it again.'

His lips touched hers lightly and then withdrew, and on an unsteady laugh, Sienna said huskily, 'Alexis, I love you. I want you. Mmm . . . Alexis?'

'Stop talking and let me love you. Let me love you now, Sienna, the way I wanted to, in my heart of hearts, that very first time I saw you, the way it should have been, the way it will be from now on.'

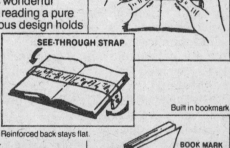

Harlequin Photo ~ Calendar ~

Turn Your Favorite Photo into a Calendar.

JULY 1984

The Browns

Uniquely yours, this 10x17½" calendar features your favorite photograph, with any name you wish in attractive lettering at the bottom. A delightfully personal and practical idea!

Send us your favorite color print, black-and-white print, negative, or slide, any size (we'll return it), along with **3** proofs of purchase (coupon below) from a June or July release of Harlequin Romance, Harlequin Presents, Harlequin Superromance, Harlequin American Romance or Harlequin Temptation, plus $5.75 (includes shipping and handling).

- -

Harlequin Photo Calendar Offer
(PROOF OF PURCHASE)

NAME_____
(Please Print)

ADDRESS_____

CITY_____ STATE_____ ZIP_____

NAME ON CALENDAR_____

Mail photo, 3 proofs, plus check or money order for $5.75 payable to:	**Harlequin Books** P.O. Box 52020 Phoenix, AZ 85072	2-5

Offer expires December 31, 1984. (Not available in Canada)   CAL-1

Take these
4 best-selling novels
FREE

as advertised on TV

Yes! Four sophisticated,
contemporary love stories
by four world-famous
authors of romance
FREE, as your
introduction to the Harlequin Presents
subscription plan. Thrill to **Anne Mather**'s
passionate story BORN OUT OF LOVE, set
in the Caribbean.... Travel to darkest Africa
in **Violet Winspear**'s TIME OF THE TEMPTRESS....Let
Charlotte Lamb take you to the fascinating world of London's
Fleet Street in MAN'S WORLD .... Discover beautiful Greece in
Sally Wentworth's moving romance SAY HELLO TO YESTERDAY.

 *The very finest in romance fiction*

Join the millions of avid Harlequin readers all over the
world who delight in the magic of a really exciting novel.
EIGHT great NEW titles published EACH MONTH!
Each month you will get to know exciting, interesting,
true-to-life people . . . . You'll be swept to distant lands you've
dreamed of visiting . . . . Intrigue, adventure, romance, and
the destiny of many lives will thrill you through each
Harlequin Presents novel.

Get all the latest books before they're sold out!
As a Harlequin subscriber you actually receive your
personal copies of the latest Presents novels immediately
after they come off the press, so you're sure of getting all
8 each month.

Cancel your subscription whenever you wish!
You don't have to buy any minimum number of books.
Whenever you decide to stop your subscription just let us
know and we'll cancel all further shipments.

Introducing

Harlequin Temptation ™.

Sensuous...contemporary...compelling...reflecting today's love relationships! The passionate torment of a woman torn between

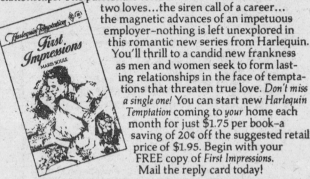

two loves...the siren call of a career... the magnetic advances of an impetuous employer–nothing is left unexplored in this romantic new series from Harlequin. You'll thrill to a candid new frankness as men and women seek to form lasting relationships in the face of temptations that threaten true love. *Don't miss a single one!* You can start new *Harlequin Temptation* coming to *your* home each month for just $1.75 per book–a saving of 20¢ off the suggested retail price of $1.95. Begin with your FREE copy of *First Impressions*. Mail the reply card today!